TYGER, TYGER

Anne Louise Bannon

Healcroft House, Publishers
Altadena, CA

Copyright

Tyger, Tyger is published by Healcroft House, Publishers, a subsidiary of Robin Goodfellow Enterprises, Altadena, California, United States of America

© 2006 Anne Louise Bannon. All Rights Reserved First Print Edition, November 2006
Second Editon, February 2105

All rights reserved. This book is a work of fiction. Any relation to real people, living or dead, is purely coincidental. No part of the book may be reproduced in any form or by any means without the prior written consent of the Author or Publisher, excepting brief quotes to be used in reviews.

ISBN # 978-0-9909923-3-2

PRAISE FOR   ANNE LOUISE BANNON

"Mesmerising. Tyger, Tyger weaves a quirky spell as Brenda and Bob search for the kidnap victim with aid from his pet Bengal tiger." —Terry L. White, author of Imagine, and The Picker.

"DEFINITELY RECOMMENDED. Combine a California animal trainer for the movies, who is in love with a school teacher afraid of commitment, with a bunch of religious fanatics in hot pursuit of a little girl and you have an exciting read!." Nancy Madison, author of Never Love a Stranger, What the World Needs Now, and Whispers, her latest popular romantic thriller.

"FAST PACED AND EXCITING. This is a modern-day high adventure interlaced with a love story, and involves a kidnapping, a tiger, and a child-at-risk. Bannon's writing never lets you down and the suspense in her story never lets up. I eagerly look forward to more books by this author."—Arline Chase, author of Killraven and the Spirit Series, Spirit of Earth, Spirit of Fire....

"WONDERFUL READING. The story moves right along. I enjoyed every word of it." — Marjorie Doughty, author of two mystery-romances, Reenactment, and Gator Hole, and the account of her adventures, living as a civilian wife in Vietnam, and Thailand duriing the 60s and 70s, Memoirs of an Insignificant Dragon.

For my mother, Connie Bannon

AMDG

Acknowledgements

I'd like to thank Alyson Rousseau, who took the picture of the tiger on the cover, and Martine Collette, both of the Wildlife Waystation in Southern California. The waystation is a shelter for wild animals, especially large cats. In addition to providing a home for these critters, from zoos, circuses and even homes that were quickly out-grown, the shelter provides education programs on much of the native wildlife in the Southern California area.

They are not open to the public except for private parties and are constantly in need of funds to help their mission. They're a 501c charity and one of the rare ones where the money goes mostly to the cause. You can like their Facebook page at WILDLIFE WAYSTATION OFFICIAL FAN PAGE or check out their website at www.WildlifeWaystation.org.

A quick shout out to the folks from the Freelance Writers who meet at the Coffee Gallery in Altadena, CA, particularly Carol Louise Wilde (whose insight made my cover possible).

Finally, thanks to my personal support team, Michael Holland and Corrie Klarner. You two make it all happen.

Did he who made the Lamb make thee?
William Blake

CHAPTER ONE

"It started when they shot my father," I told Bob.

We were strolling down Ocean Front Boulevard in Santa Monica. Not the most auspicious atmosphere for heart-wrenching confessions, but that was Bob's fault. He has this nasty habit of getting me into utterly casual settings, where I'm off my guard, then turning my guts inside out.

"Your father?" His interest picked up.

"He's not the issue," I said quickly. "The violence is."

"Oh."

It was a warm evening in July. We'd had a late dinner, and the sun was sinking into the ocean across the street, giving everything a warm orange glow.

My latest spill had Bob nodding sympathetically as he ambled along, hands in jeans pockets, with his green satin letterman jacket hanging over his elbow. Complete nonchalance. You'd think I was complaining about a stapler that didn't work instead of the violence that has dogged me for last twelve years of my life.

"I'm serious," I said.

"I know. I just don't buy your excuse is all." His arm swung out and landed on my shoulders.

"It's not an excuse. Doesn't it seem a little odd that since we've been friends, we've witnessed three armed robberies and a murder?"

"What I object to is you calling yourself a magnet for violence."

I snorted. "What else do you call it?"

"Dumb luck, engineered for a Higher Purpose, which, my dear Brenner, is not to give you an excuse for tearing yourself down and avoiding commitments."

"I'm still seeing you."

He laughed. "It's taken me two years to get this far." He suddenly stopped. "Whoa. Look at that baby."

He gazed through the window I'd just passed. It belonged to a restaurant, a mom and pop place trying to look trendy with hanging plants and a Cajun menu. Neither of the above had caught Bob's attention, though. There was a fish tank in the window, filled with live cat fish, including one old monster big enough to feed three families.

"Wonder if he's for sale." Bob's eyes gleamed as the fish wound its way around its fellows.

He had not forgotten my problem. It was merely on hold while his other passion took over for the moment. That, and Bob knows when to back off. He led me into the restaurant.

In Southern California, everyone's a hyphenate. The owner-cook-maitre d' greeted us as we came in.

Bob went straight for the fish tank.

"How much you want for the bruiser?" Bob is tricky, but rarely subtle.

"He's not for sale," said the owner-cook-maitre d'. "You'd never be able to eat that much."

"I hate fish," said Bob. "I want him for my cat. You got a pan big enough to keep him in water?"

"All that for one cat?" The man laughed. "Must be pretty big pussy. Bigger than my Hercules?"

Hercules, happily defying the Health Department, wandered out from behind a table.

2

Even accounting for the gross amounts of black and white hair, he was immense. His head, alone, was bigger than my fist.

Bob squatted and clucked. I've yet to meet the animal that could resist him. Hercules was no exception. Bob chuckled.

"He's a big one." He stroked the body. "Good muscle tone. How much for the fish?"

"Hercules couldn't eat that fish. You can't tell me your cat is bigger."

Bob shrugged and stood. "Okay, I won't. But that fish will barely make a snack for Sweetness. How much?"

I tried not to giggle. Bob loves putting people on about his cats. Not that they believe him when he tells them the truth.

"For a tale like that, fifty dollars." The owner-cook-maitre d' laughed, shaking his head.

"Great." Bob snatched his wallet, then paused. If there was more than ten dollars cash in it, I would've eaten the fish raw. He grinned sheepishly. "I wonder if my MasterCard will go through."

"Never mind." Trying not to laugh, I got out my wallet. "I'll put it on my card. You can pay me back when you get your check cashed."

"Now, Brenner, you don't have to."

"It's been a while since I spoiled Sweetness." I handed over the card. "I may as well."

I used to tease Bob about hanging around me because I kept my charge cards paid off. Until that resulted in an agonizing session over my self-image.

"So why did the violence begin with your dad?" he asked when we got back to the sidewalk. He had the pan holding the fish.

I shifted. "He was killed in a convenience store robbery. I told you that. You sure you don't want me to carry the fish?"

"You can hold it while I get the van open."

We'd been headed for Bob's van when we

stopped.

Sweetness was inside, trashing the shocks. For some reason, she let out one of her loud grumblies, scaring the shit out of a young woman passing the van. She had a firm grip on a little girl who looked like she was around five or six. Bob handed me the pan and dug out his keys.

"What is in there?" the woman gasped as Bob unlocked the back. I struggled with the catfish.

"Just my kitty," teased Bob, with a grin.

"It, uh, sounds like a lion." The woman, a rabbity looking brunette, did not want to be talking to us. Yet, she stayed, making conversation in spite of it, and the bored little girl.

"No, it doesn't. Lions roar." Bob opened the doors. "This is a Bengal tiger. Hello, Sweetness, baby."

Sweetness, at least three hundred and sixty pounds bigger than Hercules, put her massive face up against the bars across the back of the van. A tongue that could strip wallpaper flicked out and over her nose.

She'd smelled the catfish and fixed her eyes on the jiggling pan I held.

"I'd hate to have him looking at me like that," said the woman.

"Me see!" yelped the child. She wrenched her arm from the woman's grasp.

Bob put his hands out to stop her, but she approached slowly.

"Apphia!" the woman yipped, then smiled awkwardly. "She's very good with animals. We are all God's creatures, you know. There are many good lessons to be learned from tigers, if you would study the Bible, you know."

Bob kept one wary eye on Apphia, as she and Sweetness gazed at each other.

"No tigers in the Bible," said Bob, cheerfully. "I already checked, unless, you know, you treat them like lions, you know. Cats are cats, you know. And this one is hungry, aren't you, Sweetness, baby? Brenner, you want to bring Sweetness her snack?"

In the shuffle, the woman slid back from the van.

Bob maneuvered Apphia to where she could still see, but was well out of Sweetness's reach. Together, Bob and I wrestled with the aluminum pan, while he kept one shoulder on the gate. Not that Sweetness would ever bolt. But she's still a cat, and cats, if anything, are unpredictable.

The van rocked as the tiger pounced on her treat. The fish flopped around the floor while Sweetness teased it. Apphia laughed.

The woman screamed. I turned. Violence. Again.

Two men shoved the woman into a light colored Mercedes, and jumped in after her. The car was already moving as the doors slammed shut. Seconds later, I lost it in the sea of red tail lights.

Bob slammed the van doors closed, and bolted for the front.

"They're gone!" I hollered.

Apphia almost was, herself. Bob ran for the sidewalk, and caught her half a block later.

"My god, did you see that?" a female voice gasped. She had that ageless, face-lifted look you see a lot of in Southern California. "They just took her. That poor woman."

"Call the police," I snapped. I'd seen too much of this sort of thing to lose my head.

A crowd collected. Bob returned, holding Apphia's head to his shoulder. Sweetness growled loudly.

"Quiet!" Bob slapped the side of the van.

Murmurs rippled through the crowd as they tried to figure out what he had in there. It took the cops fifteen minutes to show. Most of the crowd had left by then, except the woman with the lifted face.

Her name was Florence Woodfield.

Most of the cops I know are LAPD, since that's where I usually run into my trouble. These were Santa Monica PD, since Santa Monica, contrary to popular belief, is a city unto itself. Officer J. Smalley was the senior and a woman, a no-nonsense type with short hair. Officer R. Diaz had that earnest rookie feel about him. Just what I needed.

Worse yet, there was no reason to believe a crime had taken place, only the word of three adults and a traumatized child. Apphia wouldn't say a word. It was eerie, really. She didn't cry, she didn't whimper. She just went blank, as if it didn't matter that her mother had been grabbed and taken away.

Woodfield managed to tell her tale in a reasonably coherent way, although she did say that the car was a dark Jag. Bob hadn't seen the car, and didn't say what we were doing at the back of the van. Sweetness had long since settled down, ignoring the siren when the cops pulled up. The lazy butt was probably napping.

I gave the officers the license number, and the correct details on the car.

"You think your daughter saw anything?" Smalley asked me.

"My daughter?" I asked. "Oh. Damn. No. She's not ours. It was her mom that was kidnapped."

"I was showing her my cat," said Bob. "In the back of the van. We were outside."

Smalley gave us a skeptical glare. "I thought you said you didn't know the victim."

"We'd never seen her before," said Bob. "Sweetness got noisy as we came up, and scared her. She asked what it was, and we got to talking."

"Sweetness," repeated Smalley.

"My cat," said Bob. "I'm an animal trainer. I got the permits for her. My friend has a private beach, and Sweetness likes to go swimming, so we took her down there for the day, and stopped here for dinner."

"Your cat likes to go swimming?" chuckled Diaz.

"It's not unusual for—uh..." Bob paused.

"Let's get a look in the back of that van," snapped Smalley.

"I'd better do it," said Bob quickly. "I'm not sure I locked the gate in the commotion."

He handed Apphia to me, then opened the back of the van. Sweetness was already on her feet.

"That's a tiger," Smalley said.

"They're cats." Bob locked the gate and checked it.

"Oh, my god," groaned Woodfield. "I just thought it was some weird car alarm."

"I'm an animal trainer," Bob said again. "I work big cats for the movies. Here's my card. Remember 'Would Be Adam'? Cliff Englewood's film?"

"That's that tiger!" Diaz grinned. "His name is Sweetness?"

"Her name is," said Bob. "She's quite an actress. Had even the zoo believing she was a male." He grinned nervously at Smalley. "She's really very gentle, and, believe me, I've been working big cats long enough to know you don't take chances."

Smalley bought it. Well, Bob is blonde, blue-eyed, nice shoulders and chest, with a gorgeous tight ass. The world's lucky he's so religious, because with his baby face, he'd have it made as a con man. Not that Bob was lying. He doesn't mess around when it comes to his cats, and he carries his permits with him.

"So the girl is not your daughter," said Smalley.

"No," Bob replied.

"All we know is that her name is Apphia," I said.

Apphia buried her face in my shoulder.

"Diaz, get a call out to child services for a bed," ordered Smalley. After getting Woodfield's name and address and dismissing her, the officer came over and gently touched Apphia's back.

"Apphia," she said with more kindness than I would have expected. "Honey, we know you're scared. But can you tell us your mommy's name?"

Apphia grabbed on tighter.

"Sweetheart, we want to help you," Smalley continued. "And we want to help your mommy. Can you tell us your last name?"

Apphia wouldn't budge. Smalley kept trying, and Bob tried. Even I tried. None of us could get the little waif to say a word. She didn't tremble or act scared. If she hung on Bob or me, it was more out of defiance than fear.

Unfortunately, Diaz came back with the news that the McLaren Home was filled to the rafters again.

That's where they usually put kids who've been traumatized or abused, and it would have been ideal for Apphia. The only place available was a group home in Echo Park run by a widow named Amarilla Wilson. My colleagues and I referred to her as the schoolmarm from hell. Diaz and Smalley would take Apphia there in the squad car.

Smalley turned to us. "I'll need your names and address."

"Robert Zebrinski," he said, then spelled it. "The address is on the card. Call first. I sometimes let the cats roam."

Smalley made a note. "And you, ma'am? Same name?"

"No!" I yelped. "Uh. It's Brenda Finnegan. Like the song."

Both Smalley and Diaz looked puzzled.

"I keep telling you that reference is too dated," snickered Bob.

I spelled it. Without melody.

Smalley clicked her pen. "Well, we'll hand this over to the detectives. With luck, someone will report her missing. A small kid. Somebody's bound to notice. Stay in touch."

We had to pry Apphia off of Bob. The officers put her in the car and away they rolled.

"She never asked my address," I said.

Bob's chuckle rolled out from deep in his throat.

"Ah, the misguided values of our society. She probably figured if you weren't terrified of Sweetness, you had to be living with me."

"Hm." We got in the van, and Bob pulled out. "I told you I attract violence."

"Damn it, Brenner, you teach high school in South Central LA. What do you expect?"

"You should've seen what happened when I taught in Palos Verdes. Damned senior blew his brains all over first period algebra."

"Higher Purpose. Like tonight. You stayed clear-headed, got an accurate description of the car, and the license number. Now, that poor woman has a chance." He reached over and held my hand. "It's obvious things happen to you. But you keep hiding behind that, and it's ridiculous. Okay. Your father died a violent death. You've seen a lot of violent crimes. You're scared of getting hurt. Who isn't? But, Brenner, I've survived two maulings and a major automobile accident. When I go, you can be sure God, Himself, called me, and it was my time. And if God calls me, He'll be there to take care of you."

I didn't say anything. When Bob gets religious, there isn't much to be said. It's easy for him. If he gets mauled, he can write it off to the perverse nature of cats. It's the way they are, and you don't dare take a big cat for granted, even Sweetness.

But how do you handle the pure malevolence we humans throw at each other? I never could answer that, and heaven knows, I've seen plenty of it. A perverse nature? We're supposedly intelligent beings, able to rise above our baser instincts. That may be why Bob and I get on so well. I don't dare take a human being for granted.

CHAPTER TWO

Bob woke me up the next morning. I should've turned the ringer off on my bedside phone and let the answering machine get it, but I figured it was summer, who'd be bothering me? Maybe my temporary agencies?

I temp doing bookkeeping during the times I'm not in school because I can't afford not to on a teacher's salary. People forget that we teachers don't get paid during long vacations.

But it was Bob on the phone, and not a job.

"Sorry to wake you, but I'm worried," he said. I didn't hear any cats in the background, which meant he'd already fed them.

"What else would you be?" I grumbled, or tried to. I have no idea what it sounded like. "What time is it?"

"Eight thirty."

"Eight..? Fuck! Bob!"

He wisely ignored me. "I can't stop thinking about Apphia. And Atilla the... What did you call that child services person?"

"The schoolmarm from hell. Her name's Amarilla Wilson."

Truth be told, I couldn't stop thinking about Apphia, either. Given that I work in the gang capital of Southern California, most of the little shits I turn over to child services can handle Mrs. Wilson. But Apphia. She was a waif, from her brown hair hanging about her face in thin, pathetic wisps, to her big round eyes, and bony little body. Poor little thing, stuck with Atilla the Wilson.

"There really isn't anything we can do about it, Bob," I told him through a yawn. "With her mom gone, and who knows who her father is, she had to go somewhere."

"I know. Would you mind standing character reference for me?"

I burst out laughing. "Are you out of your mind? With all your cats, you think they're going to let her anywhere near your ranch?"

"That's not fair. They're under control, and I wouldn't let her near them."

"I know that, and you know that. But I can promise you, the gang at child services is going to look at you and see two African lions, a Bengal tiger, a lynx, and a cougar."

"They're all securely caged. Apphia would stand a better chance of getting bitten by somebody's dog. Hell, even my dogs are in kennels."

Bob also raises border collies, in addition to the small domestic cats that are all over his ranch, and the cattle and sheep he keeps, plus the two horses, and the birds. It's damned near a zoo over there. Bob is about the sweetest human being on the face of this earth. He has a real weakness for foundlings. If anyone could help Apphia out of her trauma, he could.

I sighed. "Okay. I'm not promising anything. But let's do it this way. I'm friends with Janet Levy over there. I'll go talk to her, and see what I can swing. Don't count on anything. I'm telling you, St. Francis of Assisi couldn't get her with your cats."

"Brenner, you protest too much. Give me the address, and I'll meet you down there."

"Bob, I'd rather handle this, myself."

"I'll let you talk to your friend by yourself. I'll just be right there for the interview. I mean, they'll need to interview me, won't they?"

"How the hell would I know? I've never gotten anybody out. I just get them in."

I gave Bob the address, then called Janet Levy, who was very happy to make some time for me, which sucked. Not only did I have to get out of bed, I had to dress up and look respectable.

I'm not an impressive looking woman. In fact, I don't look much older than my students, in spite of a narrow face. It's not the blessing everyone seems to think. You try to face down a six foot, two-forty gang banger, and you'll see just how short 5'7" can be. I've tried the suit and hair-in-a-bun routine, but I looked ridiculous. I knew it, the kids knew it, so it's shirts and jeans, and hoping they think I'm relating to them.

As for the rest of me, well, I've got thick black hair that I usually wear in a braid down my back so I don't have to blow dry it. My blue eyes are also very near-sighted, and I wear glasses because my contacts are too much trouble. And I have freckles. Tons of them. I freckle through spf 24. My mother used to tell me I'd grow out of them, and I don't have quite so many on my face. But my freckles are mostly why I look like such a kid. Hell. I'm a math teacher. I don't have to look normal.

It took me an hour to get downtown from West Hollywood, where I live. I took the bus. I don't own a car, which is why I can afford the nice apartment in the nice secure building in the nice neighborhood. Besides, I never gave up on the ecology thing. It's nice to see it back in style.

Bob met me at the bus stop, and we exchanged the usual greetings.

"You know, I'm thinking about getting one of those Miatas," he said, watching one go past. "I'd keep my Bug, of course. But those little convertibles are great. What do you think?"

I headed for Janet's building. "They're cute.

Can you afford it?"

"Well, I've got all that money from that feature Sweetness did last June, and Jubi worked last week on that commercial, and Laxie has been out three times on the episodic." (Jubi, by the way, is pronounce you-bee, because it's short for the Latin jubilate.)

"And you've got to eat," I said. "Not to mention pay for your electricity and gas, and aren't there a couple credit card companies that want their money back? Then there's federal and state taxes. And I seem to remember one hell of a tab you ran up at the vet's last winter."

"Killjoy." Bob frowned, but he knew I was right.

Just in case anybody thinks Bob is perfect, and there are those that do, he has one major flaw: money. The man's idea of money management is to spend it while he's got it. Don't get me wrong. I'm all for spontaneity. But when you gross what Bob does, and are still hard pressed to buy lunch at McDonald's, I say there's a problem.

I will say this, since I've met him, he's got some savings and a nice little investment fund, and he lets me do his taxes. He keeps me sane. I keep him solvent. It's a perfect trade off.

Bob waited in the building lobby while I went up to Janet's office. Janet Levy and I met when she was just a case worker and I was first transferred to South Central. We've had a lot of contact over the past four years. Janet got promoted to supervisor. I still teach algebra to kids who can barely add. We occasionally get together for drinks and to bash a system that is its own greatest problem. After Bob, she's the closest thing I've got to a best friend.

"Brenda, you're looking good," Janet crowed when I walked in.

"You should talk. Look at this. A real room, with a real door that you can shut, and no mates to share it with."

Janet giggled. "You have your own room."

"Which I share with forty screaming banshees five times a day. Thank God, it's summer."

"Speaking of, why are you here?" Janet's dark brown eyes bore into me.

Anybody who writes Janet Levy off as a Jewish American Princess is begging to get laughed at. The woman is such a serious idealist… Well, hell. She's been in the child services office for eight years and will be there until she dies. She actually believes she can reach some of these gang-bangers and turn their lives around.

And she's gorgeous. Small and model thin, her skin is perfect, her teeth are naturally straight. I don't know how she does it. Between her crazy-making job and two of her own kids, by rights, she should be a wreck.

"This is kind of a tough one," I admitted. "Janet, I'm not big on asking favors. You know that. But there's a kid who got into the system last night. Her mom was kidnapped, and you guessed it, I just happened to be there."

Janet nodded. "The Jane Doe. Six years old. Light brown hair."

"Her name's Apphia."

"She says it's not."

"What?"

Janet shrugged. "She's not my case, technically. My group's adolescents. But everybody is talking about her. And what I hear is that no one, not even Dr. Marshall, can get a word out of her, except that her name is not Apphia."

"Shit. She's more messed up than I thought."

"It gets worse. She's been beaten, and some sexual abuse. Dr. Lee examined her. Going by her teeth, she's probably six, but she's seriously underweight, and traumatized, and was most likely so before the kidnapping."

I bit my lip. "What if I know somebody who can probably reach her?"

"Better than Dr. Marshall?" Janet was skeptical.

"He's a friend of mine. We were out together when it happened. In fact, we were talking with the girl and her mother. We had turned our backs when the mother was taken. The girl seemed to be responding to him. She wasn't saying anything, but she liked being with him. I spoke with him this morning before I called you. He's interested in taking custody."

"He is." Janet thought this over. "A good home environment would probably help a lot. Is he married?"

"No. But he's real stable. Owns his ranch."

"Roommates?" she asked hopefully.

"He's by himself."

Janet shook her head. "Not a prayer. She's been sexually abused, and he's a single male? They'd let her go home with Lizzie Borden sooner."

"And that's not the half of it." I got up. "He's downstairs. Would you mind coming down and giving him the bad news yourself?"

"Sure, but why?"

I glanced back at the door. "It's complicated. He may not believe me, that's all. There's... It's..."

"I'm in shock." Janet's face lit up in a huge smile. "He's your boyfriend."

"Y-yeah. We're mostly just friends. It's not that surprising that I'm seeing somebody."

Janet laughed. "It's a shock that you're telling me. It must be serious."

"Good lord, no! He's really nice, but I'm not..." I felt like such an ass. Marriage is just not my thing, and Bob knows that. It's difficult as hell to explain our relationship. Not that it's anybody's business. "Janet, come on down and meet him. This guy is so decent. The girl couldn't be safer. For crying

16

out loud, he hasn't touched me, and we've been going out for two years."

"Two years?" Janet sat back. "Are you sure you've let him?"

"Of course I have. Why would you ask such a silly thing?"

"Oh, you've only been seeing him for two years, and this is the first I've heard of it. Geez, Brenda. Why do you have to hold everybody at arm's length?"

I swallowed. "I don't do that. We're close."

Janet gave in. "All right. Sit down and tell me all about him."

"He's downstairs."

"I want to hear how you two met. What's been going on."

"Nothing," I all but groaned. "We're friends. Two summers ago, I went on a temporary assignment to do some bookkeeping for a commercial shoot. He was working it. We met, and talked, and so on. There's really not much to tell."

"What was he doing on the shoot?" Janet sat up suspiciously. "He's not an actor, is he?"

"Anything but. He's as stable as they come. He's an animal trainer. He's incredibly good with them. He can train anything. He trained an old sow for a shoot not too long ago, and he doesn't even have any pigs." I paused. "He specializes in cats."

"That's interesting. Good looking?"

I sighed. "Babe city. I can't believe a guy this good looking is hanging around me. And he's bright, and funny. And he's religious. Not snobby, self-righteous like. It's just his way of living. Believe me, he wouldn't touch this girl, except to hug her like a daddy or a brother."

Janet got up. "All right. Let's go meet this wunderkind. Honestly, Brenda. Two years?"

Janet spotted Bob in the lobby almost immediately. Bob's seat is almost always covered by nice tight jeans. The dark green satin letterman jacket isn't easy to miss either. But then Bob saw us and flashed one of his more winning smiles, and Janet had him pegged.

"Brenda, I might've known you'd understate the looks. A babe, indeed."

I ignored her. Bob met us halfway.

"Bob, this is Janet Levy," I said quickly. "Janet, Bob Zebrinski."

"It's a pleasure," Bob offered her his hand and another **200** watt smile.

"It is indeed. Brenda and I have been close friends for years."

Bob looked at me. "Really?"

Janet sniggered. "Didn't tell you about me, either?"

"Brenner tends towards a compartmentalized life."

"That's really irrelevant," I cut in quickly. "We're here to discuss the little girl."

"That." Janet sighed. "I'm afraid, Mr. Zebrinski, it wouldn't be possible for you to take the girl. I'm sure you wouldn't dream of hurting her, but being a single man living alone..."

"I understand that."

"It's stupid, really. From what Brenda told me, she was starting to bond with you. If it were in my hands, I'd say take her. But she's not my case. I only handle adolescents, and there are too many sensory judgemental tight asses who would have conniption fits if I were to suggest it."

"Sensory judgemental?" Bob asked.

"The Meyers-Briggs personality typing thing," I reminded him. "Structure freaks."

"Oh. Yeah." Bob grinned. "They would. What about a single woman? They wouldn't mind that, would they?"

"Not at all," said Janet.

"No," I said.

"She was bonding with you, too," said Bob.

"Bob, I can't. I'm not up to this."

"I'll be around to help. I haven't got a shoot scheduled for another two weeks. They'll have found her father by then. Come on, Brenner. Think of that poor little girl, all alone. Who knows what's happened to her mom. Too frightened to tell her name."

"I don't know."

Janet took my arm. "Why don't we go visit her? I'll drive you over. You, too, Mr. Zebrinski."

The scum. They knew they had me. There was a ruckus and a half going on when we got to the Wilson home. Apphia, or whatever her name was, had thrown a major tantrum. Nobody was quite sure what had triggered it. Bob got her calmed down. He played with her while I went through the paper work. I've never had more trouble signing my name in my life.

Bob drove us to my place in his Volkswagon. My place is just a basic apartment, with boring, pleasing-to-everybody, rented furniture. I move a lot and it's easier that way. He fixed lunch and I called the Santa Monica PD.

"Sergeant Griswell," answered the man I had been transferred to.

"I understand you're handling the kidnapping case from last night," I said. "I was one of the witnesses. Brenda Finnegan."

"Yep. Nothing to go on, though. The victim hasn't been reported missing. Why you asking?"

"I'm worried about her, that's all. What about the car?"

"Dead end. Must have read the numbers wrong. Owner and the neighbor swear the one with the plates you gave us was at home all night. And they're not the type to be lying. Can't say more."

"I guess not. Thank you, Sergeant." I hung up.

"What's wrong?" asked Bob.

"They checked the car out, and it was at home all night. The cops think I gave them the wrong license number."

Bob thought. "Not likely. I mean, it happened pretty quickly, but you were looking at it a long time."

"I didn't get it wrong, Bob. At least, I'm pretty sure I didn't." I looked over at the girl. "Has she said anything yet?"

"I'm Chrissie," she said, and then got louder and louder. "I'm Chrissie. My name is Chrissie. I'm Chrissie!"

"Hey, hey." Bob had her in his arms in a second. "You can be Chrissie. That's fine. We like Chrissie. Chrissie's a good name."

"Sweetness?"

"She's at home. My home. Would you like to visit?"

Crissie nodded.

"Why don't we eat some lunch first, and I'll tell you a story about Sweetness."

I set the table. Bob put the grilled cheese sandwiches out, and a bottle of ketchup. Chrissie ignored it, and sat staring. Bob put a sandwich half on her plate. She looked at him and waited.

"It's okay to eat," he said.

"Masters first," she whispered, and trembled.

"All right," said Bob, putting a sandwich on his plate. "But why don't you eat with me?"

"You won't hit me?"

"No, Chrissie. I don't hit people. Unless they hit me first. Whoops. Almost forgot to say grace. Do you say grace before eating?"

Chrissie looked bewildered. Bob made the sign of the cross. I swished through a fast sign and joined him in "Bless Us, O Lord". Under normal circumstances, we've been known to break the ten second grace, but Bob went slowly for Chrissie's sake.

She watched him, trembling, but not with fear. With anger. The child's face was perfectly
20

passive, but inside she was seething. Bob saw it, too. After a quick glance at me, we both decided to let it go, and eat. Chrissie ate neatly, but very slowly, and in the end, shoved half of her portion away. Testing us. She held her shoulders straight and defiant, as if she expected to us to beat them. Bob looked at me. I swallowed.

"If you don't want anymore, you say no thank you," I told her quietly.

That stumped her.

"Story time," announced Bob. He picked Chrissie up from the table, and swung her around to the couch. I cleaned up while he talked. "You know, Chrissie, Sweetness is just about as old as you. She's six years old. Is that how old you are?"

Chrissie nodded.

"Well, when Sweetness was just a baby tiger, she lived in India. But some bad men caught her, and put her in a box, and sent her here to America. You see, a very rich, but very stupid man had bought her. At that time, Sweetness was still small, and the man was happy with her. But Sweetness grew and grew, and the man decided that she was too big. So he wanted to kill her, and make a rug of her. A neighbor found out that the man had a real live tiger, and word got around, and I found out. I went to see the man, and I was very angry because I didn't want him to make a rug out of Sweetness. So I bought her from him, and I spent a lot of time with her, petting her, and being nice to her, so she would like me. And that's how I got Sweetness."

That's how Bob got most of his cats, except Jubi, which he inherited from his father. Bob's dad is still alive. He's a vet. He just moved up north and didn't want to bring an African lion with him.

Bob's cougar was the most recent addition. This entrepreneurial asshole with an illegal zoo had come to Bob for help because he couldn't handle Mango anymore. Bob helped him right to the Fish and Game Department, who impounded the other animals, too. Bob talked Deanna Swanson, his buddy there, into handing the cougar over to him for the trial, and Mango stayed. Bob's real good at taking in strays.

Our current stray had gone blank again. Then slowly, she began to shake, and the tears flowed. Bob rocked her.

"I want my mommy," she whispered. "I want my mommy."

CHAPTER THREE

There's not a whole lot you can do when a kid wants her mommy, and the mommy's been kidnapped. I tried to divorce myself from the whole thing, and took a long critical look at Chrissie.

She was a waif. Even her dress was a drab grey, and hung on her, making her look even more spindly. Her shoes were brown oxfords that had been patched more than once. I wondered if the damn things even fit. And now I was responsible for her.

On the counter was a scrap of paper torn from a steno pad that Bob keeps in his van. I had scrawled the license number of the getaway car on it while waiting for the police. Chrissie was still crying. I sat down next to her and Bob and put my hand on her back.

"Chrissie," I said softly. "There's not much we can do about this, but we're going to try to find your mommy."

"What?" asked Bob.

I held up the scrap. "I'm going to double check this, that's all."

"Chrissie, why don't you lay down for a second and relax. Brenner and I are going to talk." Bob got up and nodded at the back of the apartment.

All that's back there is my bedroom, but that's where we went. Bob all but slammed the door shut.

"What are you talking about, double

checking?"

"I'm just going to see who that car belongs to," I said more calmly than I felt.

"But the police already did."

"Maybe they made a mistake. I don't know. Something just doesn't feel right about what they told me and what I know happened, and they don't have the time to worry about it. Damn it, Bob, I've been through this before. You wouldn't believe the caseloads those guys have. They've got stacks of them. They're going to do whatever is easiest, and if that doesn't turn her up, they'll toss it. They have to. They have five more like it waiting."

"That doesn't mean you have to rush in."

"Yeah, well..." I looked at him helplessly. "I don't know how to explain it. It's just something I've got to do."

Bob sighed. "How are you going to do it?"

"I know someone in the DA's office. He owes me a favor."

Bob couldn't resist. "How many and how well?" he asked with a twinkle in his eye.

"I've testified for him. And that's it. He's old, fat and married, anyway."

"Come here." Bob pulled me into his arms, where it was warm and satisfying. "You need a hug. It's been a rough twenty four hours or so."

"Thanks."

He moved in for a kiss. I pulled back a little.

"Please?" he asked. "I can't help it, Brenner."

I let him. I shouldn't have. Bob's kisses are wonderful and have this nasty way of turning me inside out.

"We'd better get going," I said when I could. "I want to get Chrissie some new clothes before we go out to your place."

"Good idea." Bob got out his wallet. "I cashed that check this morning."

I turned on him. "All of it?"

"Well, I put half in savings."

"And you're walking around with six thousand dollars in cash." I shook my head. "Hand it over."

He did. "I really appreciate this. Why don't you buy Chrissie's clothes with some of it? And take out for the fish last night, too."

"I will. We'll go by your bank, first."

Chrissie calmed down while I talked Nolan Casey, of the District Attorney's office, into finding out who owned the car I had the license number for. I had to tell him the whole story first.

"Well," he said slowly. "Your interest is legit, I'll give you that much. But I need a docket number for the application. Those aren't public records."

"For crying out loud, you're a DA. Can't you just tell them you're trying to build a case?"

There was a pause. "I'll see what I can do. Keep in mind, it takes them up to ten days to get it back from Sacramento."

"I'll keep my machine on. Call me the minute you get it. And thanks a lot, Nolan. I really appreciate it."

"Just don't do anything dangerous."

"I won't. Thanks again."

Chrissie was really well-behaved in the bank, unnaturally so. She kept her eyes straight ahead of her at all times, and if she was curious, she didn't say so.

We got Bob squared away in record time.

The Westside Pavillion completely flummoxed Chrissie. She tried to keep her eyes straight ahead, but little furtive glances kept slipping out. Bob knelt beside her.

"It's something else, here, isn't it?" he said gently.

"Want to ride on my shoulders so you can see better?"

She frowned. "I can look?"

"Sure," said Bob. "That's what a mall is for. There's all sorts of neat things to see here."

After that, Chrissie's head didn't stop swivelling.

At the children's store we had to get a clerk to help us. All I remembered about kids clothes was that when I was six I wore a six-x. Back to school clothes were already out, and it was only July. Chrissie seemed bewildered by all the different styles.

"Colors are bad," she finally told me in the dressing room.

"Who told you that?" I asked.

"The masters."

"And who are the masters?"

"The masters," Chrissie insisted.

Some sort of authority figures, I guessed.

"Well," I said. "They're not in charge here. I am, and I say you can wear any pretty colors you like."

Chrissie still found it hard to pick out clothes, so I ended up making the decisions. I also had her wear a new shorts set out of the store. While I was paying for everything, Chrissie spotted a lady who was painting personalized barrettes. The little girl watched gravely.

"Do you want your name on a barrette?" Bob asked.

Chrissie nodded. The lady painted a pair in those cutesy dot letters with little flowers on them. Chrissie was enchanted and showed it to me proudly.

I was a little preoccupied. She needed everything, underwear, socks. I had no idea little kids wore so much, or cost so much. By the time we were done, Bob's Miata was more than a couple hundred dollars further away. But Chrissie had shoes that fit (the oxfords had been too small), enough clothes to get through a week, underwear, a sweater, and another set of barrettes. I brushed her fine hair into a pony tail, and clipped in the name barrettes. She was still a waif, but a well dressed one.

We also bought her some candy and a teddy bear.

She clamped the bear to her chest, and would not give it up, even to get in the car.

It was getting on for three o'clock when we finally pulled up to the gate in front of Rancho Assisi. St. Francis is Bob's favorite saint. He's got a couple hundred acres tucked into a canyon up near Tujunga.

It's absolutely gorgeous, with brown rolling hills dotted by thick stands of oak. His parents bought it years ago for their retirement when Bob was a kid, then sold it to him for dirt cheap and moved up north.

Parked on the road outside was a blue mini-pickup. Bob got the automatic gate opener going, then stopped the Bug just in the drive and got out.

A tall, jeans-clad, cowboy-booted man slid out of the truck and ambled over. They exchanged handshakes. Bob got back in the car, and pulled it into what passes for a carport on his property.

"Dr. Stevenson," Bob explained briefly. "He's that zoologist that's studying my cats."

"Yeah, you told me."

The blue pickup had followed us through the gate, and now pulled around to the back, where the cages are. Bob helped Chrissie out of the car.

"Okay, Chrissie. We can go back and look at my cats, but you stay away from the cages. You just look, and don't get anywhere near them. You're just the right size for a big cat toy, and the cats might try to play with you, and they'll hurt you without meaning to. Okay?"

Chrissie nodded. I still held her hand.

Around back, the lions were roaring happily, and the other cats were growling, and chuffing and making their various greeting noises. Dr. Stevenson ambled along the row of cages, hands in back pockets, nodding. He looked up as we came around the house.

"Looking good, Bob," he announced as he

joined us.

"Thanks." Bob pushed me forward. "Brenner, this is Dr. Mel Stevenson. Mel, my girlfriend, Brenner."

I felt like kicking Bob. Instead, I murmured the usual pleasantries and shook hands.

"And this is Chrissie, Brenner's houseguest."

Chrissie clung to Bob. Bob chuckled.

"She's a little shy. Have you gotten a look at the cougar yet?" Bob handed Chrissie to me, and headed for the cage at the far end of the row. "His name's Mango. He's not warming up at all. I'm pretty sure Atkins was mistreating him."

Bob chirped and clucked as he came up to the snarling cougar. Mango hissed and put his ears back at Dr. Stevenson, then let up as Bob's soft voice calmed him.

"It's a crying shame," said Bob as Dr. Stevenson looked on. "We'll never be able to work him. I'd let you in the cage, but Chrissie—Aw, shit!"

This last was said softly. Chrissie had slipped from my grasp and walked slowly towards Sweetness's cage. The tiger saw her coming and walked up to the bars. Bob moved quickly, but with a smooth sort of grace that wouldn't arouse the cats.

Chrissie stopped about ten feet in front of the tiger and sat down. Sweetness sat down also. The two just stared at each other.

Bob stopped. We looked at each other for some explanation, and found none. Dr. Stevenson took notes. Sweetness chuffed-chuffed.

"They seem to like each other," said Dr. Stevenson. "How much contact has this child had with Sweetness?"

"Just last night," said Bob.

"Any petting?"

"Are you kidding? I wouldn't take a chance like that."

Not when Sweetness could break Chrissie's

arm just saying hi. Dr. Stevenson nodded. Bob went over to Chrissie and whispered in her ear. She got up and followed him into the house.

"We can look at the cats again later after he's done," Bob said as we went in. He stopped in the doorway and yelled outside. "I've gotta check my messages, and I'll be right out."

Bob's house is a basic ranch style with two bedrooms and a den. Both the master bedroom and the living room have sliding glass doors to the back, but Bob usually goes in and out through his huge kitchen.

It's the biggest room in the house because it's also the dining room, and Bob needed the extra space for the walk-in freezer where he stores the meat for his cats.

Bob's trained small cats came running in. There are five of them that Bob uses on shoots, and they stay indoors. Actually, there are six that stay indoors.

Rambo, a black and white short hair, was not responding to training. Bob had brought him in because he was teasing the big cats, and it was only a matter of time before one of them sent Rambo to that big scratching post in the sky.

Bob settled Chrissie in a kitchen chair, gently knocked Rambo off the table, then hit the button on the answering machine. The kitchen phone is next to the den, and the answering machine is part of the same unit. It beeped.

"Hi, Bob, it's Wes," the machine announced. "Listen, I got a great gig for you."

Bob went to the refrigerator for some milk.

"...It starts in September. I need a wrangler for some cattle scenes."

"Can I help?" I asked.

Bob shook his head, and made a note.

"...We'll be shooting in the Dakotas somewhere. Hey, I know you don't want to leave your cats, but this is big bucks, and it'll only be for three weeks. Get your girlfriend to feed them."

I grimaced. "Will you please stop telling everyone I'm your girlfriend?"

Bob got out a box of Quik and chuckled.

"...Anyway, give me a call back as soon as you can. I gotta have an answer by Thursday. Bye."

"Well, what are you, if you aren't my girlfriend?" Bob asked.

Beep. "Bob? It's Sue. I got that episodic. Steady bucks for a change. Great, huh? Anyway, we need that hill behind your place."

Bob made another note. "You're not seeing anybody else. I'm not seeing anybody else. We hug, we kiss."

"...We're talking money, although I know you'll give me a decent break. That's what big brothers are for. Beep me the second you hear this—310-555-8872."

I snorted and ignored him.

Beep. "Hi. This is Jim Donahue, Elixer Productions—818-555-4716."

Bob's eyebrows lifted. "Again?" He stopped making chocolate milk long enough to make another note.

"...We'll need your lynx, uh, Laxie, for two days the first part of next week. Uh, Monday and Tuesday, the 22nd and 23rd. Please call to confirm. Same rate. Uh, bye."

"They're using Laxie a lot," I said.

Beep. Silence. From the machine, that is. The six cats noisily let us know they wanted some attention.

"It's that detective soap that started last spring," said Bob. "It went surrealistic."

Whoever had called, had decided not to leave a message. The machine clunked with a phone hanging up.

"The lynx is supposedly some deified source

of inspiration for the detective." Bob put a glass of chocolate milk in front of Chrissie.

Beep. "Bob, it's Deanna."

"Shit!" For the first time, the answering machine had Bob's full attention. Deanna was Deanna Swanson from the Fish and Game Department, and her calls often meant a raid.

"…I'm just checking up on the cougar. I'm so glad you got him. Call me when you get a chance. Also, I talked to Ralph MacMillan at the zoo, and he mentioned that he's got some vitamin supplements. He said if you're interested to give him a call. Talk to you later."

"Whew," Bob muttered.

Beep. "Bob, it's Sue. Where are you? The director looked at the shots of your place and he wants it big time. You may not have to give me a break. He wants the cattle, too, and he wants you to wrangle them, and he wants an answer yesterday. Beep me. Now. Bye."

Bob went to the back door. "Mel? How's it going?"

He waited. "Fine. I got some calls to make. I'll be out in a bit." He turned to me. "You have any problems with Chrissie watching TV while I get these calls and Mel squared away?"

"I guess not. Come on, Chrissie. Bring your milk."

Rambo and Flat Cat, a seal point Siamese, were both on the table. Bob squirted them with his pump bottle. Flat Cat scrambled off and tore around the kitchen. Rambo shook his head and glared at Bob.

Bob removed Rambo to the floor.

Chrissie gazed at the TV in rapture as I turned it on. Flipping through the channels turned up the Disney Channel. I vaguely remembered Sue mentioning that they'd turned over to a regular cable from a pay channel. Bob only had the cable because reception was lousy in the canyon, and didn't pay for any of the premium channels. I shrugged and figured that was as safe as anything else and left it on.

Rambo followed us in, although he was after Chrissie's milk. Theodora ambled in and laid down with her head in Chrissie's lap. Theo is extremely friendly, which is the last thing you'd expect from a high-class white Persian. Arabella, a long hair calico, with white front paws and belly, skittered in and decided that Chrissie needed mothering. Chrissie ignored the cats.

When I got back to the kitchen Bob was telling Deanna that Mango was doing just dandy and that Dr. Stevenson was there. Sanders, a grey short hair, and Flat Cat danced and rubbed themselves against Bob's shins, while Sir Toby Belch, a long hair grey tiger cat, sat and glared. Sir Toby rarely deigns to have anything to do with the other cats, or anyone else for that matter, unless there are treats involved.

Some minutes later, Bob had confirmed Laxie with Jim Donahue, left a message on Wes's machine and beeped Sue, got her call, and agreed to meet with the director at the house at five. He sighed as he hung up the phone for the last time.

"Why does everything have to happen during the height of the shooting season?" he asked me.

"Be thankful. The busy little ants have safely summer's bounty away, and next January, when nobody's shooting squat, you'll still be eating."

"I'm so glad you're the practical type. I gotta get outside."

"Fine. I'll go work on your books."

I got everything from the den, plus the receipts from earlier and brought them into the living room.

Chrissie was transfixed by the television, but still solemn. Rambo slept on top of the TV. Arabella sulked from under the bookshelf. Outside, I could see Bob letting each big cat out of its cage so Dr. Stevenson could look it over. I sat down in the easy chair, and Theodora came over to nap in my lap.

I had been working a while, and was completely absorbed in it, when I looked up to rest my eyes.

Chrissie was no longer in front of the TV. I panicked for a second until I saw her. Outside, Bob and Dr. Stevenson were talking quietly and watching.

Chrissie sat about three feet from the sliding glass door, staring at a sitting Sweetness on the other side, who stared right back at her.

CHAPTER FOUR

Sue's director arrived at six thirty. It figured. The more industry types want something, the later they show up to get it. I fed Chrissie while Bob took the director to look over the hills behind the house.

We put Chrissie to bed in the guest room as soon as the director left. I had suggested going home, but Bob said he wanted to talk to me.

"She's asleep," I said, coming into the living room. "So what's up?"

Bob sat on the couch, thumbing through a concordance.

"Apphia, Apphia. Here it is." He traded the bible index for a real bible and flipped through the pages.

"There's only one reference. Paul's letter to Philemon. Here it is. It's part of the greeting."

"What are you talking about?" I shooed Saunders off the love seat and sat down.

"The name Chrissie's mom called her. I was thinking it might be a biblical name, and it is."

"So?"

He picked up the concordance. "That produces or is fruitful. That's what Apphia means. It makes sense. The sexual abuse, the zombie-style obedience, masters. Remember how dowdy her mom looked?"

"Now that I think about it, she did have a pretty ugly dress on. I don't get it."

"They belong to a cult, obviously a

34

very repressive one, and one that emphasizes evangelization."

Bob shut the book and toyed with the cover.

"Chrissie's mom did not want to talk to us, but seemed to feel she had to, and brought up the Bible almost immediately."

I thought about it. "You're right. Only, why was she kidnapped? It couldn't be the cult. If she was trying to convert you, then she wasn't running away, and even then, they would have grabbed Chrissie, too."

"That's assuming they could have reached her. Or held onto her. She's pretty slippery."

"No shit." Theodora jumped into my lap, and I absently scratched between her ears. "What if Chrissie's mom wasn't really kidnapped? The other cult people were just taking her back, maybe punishing her for not holding onto Chrissie, who was running away."

"Then it's possible they didn't see her when they grabbed her mom."

"So if we find the cult, we find her mom." I sat back. "In which case, do we have a right to keep Chrissie out of there? However much we don't like it, it is their religion, and they have a right to practice as they like."

"What if they're keeping her mom against her will?"

"But she wasn't running away."

"What if she wants to now?"

I sighed. "I suppose we should see if we can find the cult. That ought to be a lead pipe cinch."

Bob yawned and got up. "They may yet find us first. I'm not exactly thrilled about sending Chrissie back to that environment." He put his books on the shelf where they belonged, then sat down next to me.

"Why don't we give them a little time to come calling? In the meantime..."

He snuggled up, and I not only let him, I

snuggled back. My insides notwithstanding, getting cuddly with Bob had considerable appeal. The necking was lazy and delicious.

"Why don't you spend the night?" he whispered after a while.

I smiled. "I have been waiting so long for you to ask me that."

"I'll sleep out here on the couch. You can have my bed."

"And you call me a killjoy."

Bob's lips tickled my ear. "Are you going to make a commitment to me?"

My lip curled. "Why are you so hung up on that?"

"Because you're so hung up on not." He wriggled around and held my face. "Brenner, I can't even tell you I love you without you going all cold and freaked out on me. That's no way to make love."

"Want to make a bet?" I pushed him backwards and kissed his lips hard.

Bob shoved back. "You get mad when I tell people you're my girlfriend, and you didn't tell your closest friend we were seeing each other until today. Let's be honest, are you really interested in waking up afterwards?"

I wanted to say I was, but we both knew it was a lie.

The lions woke me up the next morning around six thirty, roaring for their breakfasts. I tried going back to sleep and lasted until seven when the dogs joined the "feed me" chorus. Both Bob and Chrissie had been up for an hour or so. Chrissie was eating cereal as I stumbled into the kitchen. The teddy bear sat next to her. From the looks of it, she'd held onto it through a bath. I mumbled hello to her, but she didn't respond.

Bob greeted me with a happy good morning and a big hug and kiss that kept getting bigger. Finally freed, I stumbled for the coffee maker.

"Will you help me feed the animals?" he asked, opening the refrigerator.

"If you'll wait a couple minutes for the caffeine to kick in."

Bob whistled Ode to Joy as he hacked up a beef joint for the cats.

"What's with you?" I asked, trying not to snarl.

"What do you mean?"

"You slobbered all over me, you're whistling Beethoven. You're not usually such a cheery riser."

"I've had my coffee." He was evading me.

"Yeah, right. Something's up."

"Nothing's up."

"Yes, there is. What is it?"

"I can't tell you."

"Don't give me that."

"You'll get mad at me."

"Oh." I knew what that meant.

Bob was in one of his euphoric moods, which, as he tried to tell me before he knew better, were brought on by overwhelming feelings of love for me.

I shuddered.

He nuzzled up to me sideways so he didn't drip gore on me and nibbled on my ear.

"Let's just say my heart's greatest desire is being fulfilled this morning."

I tried to glare at him. "I haven't had my coffee yet."

Bob chuckled and went back to hacking and whistling. Chrissie had disappeared. I got up and went to the window.

"Oh, my god," I gasped. "Chrissie's outside."

"I told her she could," said Bob calmly. "She knows to stay away from the cages, and I've been keeping an eye on her."

"She's staring at Sweetness again."

Bob looked out the window also. Chrissie sat about ten feet away from the Sweetness's cage, the tiger sat at the bars, and the two stared at each other.

"Chrissie is awful small," I said. "Could Sweetness be thinking prey?"

Bob shook his head. "That's not her hungry look. They just like each other, I guess. It's the weirdest thing I've ever seen. I'd better get her in."

We got Chrissie safely indoors, and shooed away the little cats. Bob fed his dogs while I carefully opened each large cage, put in a pan, patted the big cat inside, and quietly exited. I stopped at the cougar cage. Bob had finished with the dogs by then.

Clucking and chirping, he slid Mango's food in through the small feed gate. For once, Mango didn't hiss at him. Bob cooed and clucked, whispering Mango's name as the cat ate. One of the first things Bob does when he gets a cat that's been mistreated is change its name so it isn't constantly reminded of bad things.

"Come on over, Brenner," he said softly. "He may as well get used to you, too."

"That's real reassuring, Bob." I joined him next to the cage.

His hand slowly slid through the bars and petted Mango. The cat ignored him.

"I'm on a roll today," he whispered.

"I thought you said you'd never be able to tame him."

"Oh, I'll tame him up. But I'll never be able to work him. He'll always be too unpredictable and dangerous. I'll probably have to sell him to a zoo, or maybe the wild animal park. It's a pity. He's a good looking cat." He pulled his hand away, and grinned at me. "You want to work Sweetness while I'm cleaning her cage?"

"It's better than cleaning up tiger turds. But I thought you wanted me to work Laxie so I can take him on that shoot Monday."

"No. I want to work with you while you work Laxie. But Sweetness wants her cage cleaned, and you might as well warm up on her."

Thrilling. Bob had been training me for about a year on the theory that if I was going to be hanging around him it would be better if I could handle his babies. He's lost a few girlfriends that way. They didn't get hurt. They chickened out, and the one that didn't is now his biggest competitor.

Neither was likely to happen to me. As far as I'm concerned, big cats aren't nearly as dangerous as gang members and junkies, and I get my fill of the entertainment industry working office temporary in the summer. And working Sweetness at that moment had its disadvantages. She was going through a testing phase with me.

I let her out of her cage, and the first thing she did was walk straight over to sliding glass door that led to the living room, and sit down in front of Chrissie.

I looked over at Bob. He was equally bemused.

"She can't smell Chrissie through the glass, can she?" I asked.

"Nah," said Bob.

"And you told me tigers don't see that well."

"She probably recognizes the shape." Shaking his head, he went back to sweeping up turds.

Bob had a basic routine he wanted me to put Sweetness through. I had a hell of a time getting her to budge. Then the bitch charged me. It's a little unnerving to have three hundred and ninety two pounds of Bengal tiger coming at you. I managed to stand my ground and shout her into submission. After that she was pretty well-behaved, although she kept one eye turned toward the living room.

We worked with Laxie, the lynx, for another hour.

Laxie is a lot easier to deal with, because although he is technically a big cat and a wild animal, he only weighs thirty six pounds, and stands two feet at the shoulder. He still gets stubborn, and his teeth make him plenty dangerous, but it's much easier to physically move him.

The morning was getting hot. Bob's house and main yard are pretty well shaded by trees, so he doesn't need air conditioning. Still, between the exertion and summer heat, I was sweating like a horse. I'm not allowed to say sweating like a pig because, as Bob pointed out, pigs don't sweat, and it's not fair to them.

Anyway, I needed a shower badly, and I wanted to get into some fresh underwear. Bob wanted to keep Sweetness and Chrissie bonding, so he packed the tiger into the van, took Chrissie and me back to my place, then ran over to the zoo.

I stopped at the mail boxes and opened mine.

Nothing but bills and junk mail. I started for my place and almost bumped into my neighbor.

"Hey, you live next door," he said cheerfully.

"Yeah. Nice to meet you." I tried to push onward.

"Nice kid. Relative?" He followed me.

"Friend."

"Say, you're a real popular lady."

I turned on him. "What?"

"I thought you were having a party last night. Someone kept buzzing your lobby phone until about eleven."

"I wasn't home. Thanks for telling me." I hurried Chrissie up the stairs.

He followed. "I haven't had much of a chance to talk to you since you moved in."

"I've been busy."

"Yeah, well, maybe it's time we got to know each other. Good neighbors, and all, you know."

I gave him a weak grin. "Well, maybe my boyfriend and I can have you over one evening."

His interest dimmed. "Yeah, sure."

I unlocked my door and held it open for Chrissie.

40

A half wave, and I was inside. People say you can live ten years in Los Angeles and never learn your neighbor's name. That's a big not for me. No matter where I move, my neighbors always start nosing around. I'd been in that place for five months, and already it was looking like time to move.

The lobby phone buzzed while I was stepping out of the shower. I broke my neck trying to get it, but whoever had hung up. It wasn't Bob. He would have waited.

I was dressed and trying to figure out lunch when the lobby phone buzzed again.

"Miss Finnegan?" asked an unfamiliar voice.

"May I ask who's calling?"

"I'm here for Apphia."

"Really? What's your name?"

"Would you please bring her down?"

"Give me your name, I'll get it verified with child services, and then we'll talk."

The man hung up. I debated rushing downstairs, but knew I'd never catch him. The regular phone rang anyway.

"Brenner, I'm still at the zoo. Want to meet for lunch at that Chinese place on Beverly?"

"Mandarette? I suppose. I think I can get a bus down La Cienega, or maybe I'll try Fairfax. Hang on a minute while I play with schedules."

I got so absorbed working with the MTA that I completely forgot about the lobby call. LA's bus system can do that to you. They made the first attempt while Chrissie and I waited at the bus stop.

There were two of them, both young men, dressed in suits they got off the sale rack at K-mart. They stepped up next to Chrissie. She clung to me, and I moved away. One reached.

"Touch that kid, and I'll scream so loud those cops over there will drop their doughnuts."

The men moved back. I got a good grip on Chrissie and turned to them.

"Give me your names, and we'll talk," I told them. "I can't turn her over without proof you've got the right to take her. But I'll talk, and we can get it worked out with child services."

They looked over at the cops nervously. I waited.

The bus pulled up.

"Have it your way," I said, boarding with Chrissie in tow. "See ya."

They must have followed us in their own car.

There was a tight connection when we changed buses at Fairfax, and a pair of cops writing somebody up when we changed again at Beverly. The bus dropped us off across the street from the restaurant. Bob's van was out front. There was no place close for them to park, so the men didn't catch us until we hit the corner.

I saw one out of the corner of my eye. I always travel with my keys in hand. I swung for him, but fell over Chrissie. The keys and my glasses went flying. She scrambled up and took off running. The first guy's partner ran after her. I wrestled with the guy I had tried to hit.

That son of a bitch was strong. It did take him a few minutes, and I got in a couple good punches, but he got me in a headlock with his hand in my hair. He yanked me to my feet. And let go. Sweetness sat calmly on the sidewalk and snarled.

Bob had her on a lead. He had pulped the guy and made sure Chrissie was in the van before letting Sweetness out. The pulped guy staggered up.

"You are damned," he told us through a fat lip. "The child is ours."

"So get it cleared through children's services," I said, giving his partner a shove. I picked up my glasses. Blood trickled down my knee, and I ached all over.

"The people of which you speak are corrupt agents of a demon government."

I had to smirk. "Or are you too afraid they'll file abuse charges?"

"We are caring for her immortal soul! The child has been rescued and cleansed. She has been under the influence of this world for too long already. Would you condemn her?"

Bob shook his head. "Look, guys, I know you're worried about her, and I respect that. But I don't see her running to your open arms, and there is evidence of abuse, and all we have is your word that she belongs with you. Get it cleared with children's services, and the kid is yours. Until then, Sweetness, grr."

Sweetness snarled again and pawed the air. The men backed off. Bob hurried Sweetness into the van, gave her some treats, and told her what a good baby she was.

We tried to follow the dark blue seventies Caprice, but lost it somewhere in Hollywood.

"Think they knew you were cueing Sweetness?" I asked as we looked for them.

Bob shrugged. "Does it matter?"

"It might. If they think she's tame, they might try to get around her."

"Let 'em."

I looked at him, surprised by his venom.

CHAPTER FIVE

Wednesday afternoons are my time with the shrink, something else that Bob is responsible for. You'd think in eighteen months we would have gotten somewhere. Dr. Robbins just says that there is no time as far as the subconscious is concerned. In the meantime, I'm paying off his mortgage.

I shouldn't say that. It has been helping. Just look at how much I've opened up to Bob.

Dr. Robbins seemed a lot more interested in my interest in Chrissie than he was in taking care of her. It made sense. Dr. Robbins doesn't work with children. He did watch her play with Bob, and came to the same conclusion Bob had. We agreed to talk to Dr. Marshall about it, and that was about it. I didn't even get to do my usual round of blaming everything on my mother.

Bob was pretty tense. He took us back to my place, but he wasn't happy about it. We put Chrissie in front of the TV and went into the bedroom.

"Have you heard at all from children's services?" he asked as I picked up my bedroom phone.

"I'm calling them now." I dialed, listened to recorded instructions, pressed extension numbers, and talked over it all. "I didn't have any messages on my machine when I got here this morning, and I haven't got any now."

"Then how did they know about you?"

"Janet Levy, please." I told the secretary.

"That's what I'm trying to find out. Janet, this is Brenda."

"Hello. How's it going with the little girl?"

"Pretty well. She's decided her name is Chrissie, so that's what we're calling her. Do you know if anybody has turned up to claim her?"

"We haven't heard from a soul. I've been checking myself. Why?"

"A couple guys in cheap suits showed up today demanding I hand her over. We have reason to believe Chrissie was raised by an off the wall religious cult, and these guys are trying to get her back. We told them to go through you."

"Did you say cheap suits?"

"Yeah. Dark colored, tailored by the polyester twins."

"I'll be damned. I saw them as you guys left yesterday, or something like them. It looked like they were following you, but I thought it was just my imagination. I'm really wondering now."

"No shit. That might explain it. All they had to do was pick my mail box to get my name, especially if they saw me open it yesterday."

"Brenda, do you want me to call the police?"

"No. Bob and I managed to scare them off. I think we can handle it ourselves. I doubt they'll be back, anyway. I'll be in touch. Thanks."

Bob glared at me as I hung up. "Well?"

I told him what Janet had said. "Those guys probably were going to get Chrissie when they saw us, and then thought they wouldn't have to deal with the demon government."

"That settles it." Bob paced the room. "You're not safe here. We'll go back to my place. I'll turn on the fence, and let the cats roam tonight. Even if they track me down, they won't try anything. Nobody's that stupid."

"And if they have guns?"

Bob winced. "They can't shoot them all. And

there is the electric fence. If they get through that, the sheriff's department should be there by then."

"Okay." I looked everywhere but Bob. "I suppose I should go, too."

"Brenner, don't think for a second that I am leaving without you." There was a tightness in his voice, and I knew what it was, and it gave me the heebee-jeebies.

Unfortunately, Bob was right. About the danger. I packed an overnight case, and put Chrissie's clothes in a grocery bag. We both looked for cars following us, but found nothing. I had Bob stop at the library, where I photocopied the church listings in every phone book for Southern California.

"Are you going to call every one of these?" asked Bob, as he helped.

"Only the weird ones, and I'll start with the ones in Santa Monica."

"The one we want is probably not listed."

"They're big on evangelization. They just might be."

"How are you going to know you've got the right one?"

"I don't know yet. But I'm doing something. I hate just sitting around waiting for things to happen."

Bob, of course, could. The man has infinite patience. He'd have to hanging around me as long as he has.

At the ranch, we dropped the suitcases while Bob got Sweetness caged up. I helped Bob drop a roll of chain link, some wire and some barbed wire, and a tool case into the bed of his pickup. Bob saddled up one of his horses, a black mare named Princess. I got the border collies, Chi-Chi, Morroco, and Lady, into the back of the truck. Chrissie rode shotgun as I drove around the perimeter of the ranch, while Bob trotted along behind. There weren't any holes, which wasn't surprising. Bob keeps a pretty good eye on his fence.

As we went around, Bob began rounding up his cattle and sheep. We drove slowly, which was the only reason Bob let the dogs in the back. They jumped out at the first cow we ran across.

Bob has between forty and sixty head of hoof stock. Being herd animals, they do tend to hang together, in a spread out sort of way. So rounding them up is not as difficult as one might think, given how much land Bob has.

It's amazing to watch him. He uses a whistle, a horse and three dogs, and that's all to control sixty really stupid sheep and cows ready to panic if a fly lands wrong. The collies are pure poetry. The whistle blows, and Lady and Morroco are off running, barking at three cows. Chi-Chi drops to her belly and creeps, until the whistle brings her to her feet, daring the cows to come any closer.

After we were sure the fence was secure, the round up began in earnest. I took the pick up ahead to the big holding barn and opened the gates. It seemed like forever before Bob and the animals arrived. I was about to go after him, when I heard the rumble of hooves, and mooing and baaing, and dogs yipping.

The dogs separated the sheep from the cattle and herded them each into their side of the barn.

Bob counted heads before I shut the doors.

"That should be all of them," he said.

I bolted the doors. "If not, the cats will have a snack tonight, assuming they remember to eat it."

Being well-fed, they didn't always. I smiled at him.

His return smile was halfhearted.

It was my turn to cook dinner. I personally find it a dreary chore, especially for myself. On the other hand, I'm not a bad cook, and Bob is an appreciative eater. Chrissie sat in the living room watching Sweetness watch her.

"Next Thursday," Bob said into the phone. "I'm pretty sure I can swing it. What exactly are we talking about?... Uh huh.... Uh huh.... What group?... Oh, him.... I want to hear the song before I commit, and it's gotta be MOS.... My cats don't go out on any of that satanic stuff, period.... Not any that are mellow enough to do what you want, and it will be MOS, or not at all.... I might be able to get one of my lions to put up with it.... Well, Sweetness is the most mellow tiger in the state, but she won't put up with that heavy metal crap.... Ten k, and not a penny under.... Fine, get another cat, if you can.... Look, you want a complicated routine, and physical contact with some bozo who trashes guitars. Five to one this clown can't handle domestic cats. I've got my insurance to think about. It's ten k, or forget it.... I'll confirm it when I've heard the song.... Right. Thanks. Bye."

I smiled as he hung up. "Coming out of the woodwork for a change."

"It's been busy." Bob stretched.

"Better watch it, you'll have to start paying taxes."

"You accountant types all think alike." Bob snuggled up.

"So who's him?"

"Who? Oh, the video. It's for Josh Ragner. They want him playing with Sweetness. I hope like hell he isn't a stoner."

"It might be better if he is."

"At least it's not a rap video. Damn, I hate that stuff."

"You hate heavy metal, too."

"Yeah, but I can make them turn off the playback when it's metal because it upsets the cats. They actually seem to like rap." He smiled. "And you actually seem to like me."

"Like is irrelevant. Will you please unhand me and dry the lettuce?"

Bob let go. He looked at me for a moment, then bent to his task. He was worried, and there was a sadness in that look. It made me feel guilty for everything I was not.

Chrissie did not want to come to dinner. Like Sweetness, she was going into a testing phase, too. I was under contract not to employ corporal punishment. After a minute of stubborn sulking, I wanted to dump the contract. I settled for giving her a choice of going to bed right then, or coming to the table. She chose bed.

It was tense at the table. There were domestic cats all over the place, as we shooed every one in that we could find. Bob was sullen, although he agreed with me on the discipline thing. And he was worried about his cats getting shot by a bunch of fucked up religious fanatics. I was worried, too, mostly about him.

"I'll clean up," I told him as we finished eating.

"Nah. I'll help." He got up, and I with him.

I put my hand on his shoulder. "It'll be all right, Bob. If the cult is that cruel, child services will not let them have Chrissie back."

"Brenner..." He squeezed my hand, then pulled me into a strong hug. Just barely trembling, he held me for a long time. "Do you know any self-defense stuff?"

"Enough to keep from getting creamed by gang bangers." I smiled at him, then pulled away. "You don't have to worry about me, Bob."

"Then will you forget about playing private eye?"

"Why? I'm just making a few phone calls."

"Trying to locate people who beat the crap out of you this afternoon."

"I tripped over Chrissie. And the worst that happened is my knees got scraped. You don't seem to mind me working your cats, and they can do a hell of a lot worse."

Bob pressed his lips together. "You know

49

what my cats are going to do. Those cult crazies are impossible to predict. Why can't you let the police handle it? That's what we pay taxes for."

"They don't have time." Feeling a little angry myself, I concentrated on putting the leftover greens into the waste bag for the compost heap, and collecting the meat and fat scraps for the dogs. The bones would be dried for bone meal, which Bob sold to a garden products company. He does not believe in wasting anything. "And maybe I need to do this. Maybe it's my way of making up for all the violence. I've always just sat back and watched it happen. For once, I'm going to do something about it." I looked at him. "I have to. It's just something I've got to do."

I turned back to the dishes. Bob came up behind me and pressed me close to him.

"Brenner, please don't get mad at me. I can't help it. I'm worried about you. I'm afraid you're going to get hurt. If something happened with the cats, I'd be able control it, stop it from happening. I can't control these cult people." He paused, struggling. "I can't control you, either, and I'm not going to try. You have to do what you think is best. I'll be around to help. Just please don't get mad at me when I get afraid for you."

I wanted to be flip, to say he shouldn't tell me about it, then. I wanted to reassure him, to say that it meant a lot to me that he cared so much. I wanted to beg him to protect me, and I wanted to tell him to leave me alone. I didn't say anything, and went back to cleaning the dishes.

Once the kitchen was clean, I went to the guest room to check on Chrissie. Bob had gotten out a sleeping bag and air mattress for her. He has a double bed in there, so Chrissie and I could have slept together.

But Chrissie had wet the bed the night before. Bob didn't think I wanted to sleep with that. And the sleeping bag could be tossed in the washer in the morning. It's harder to do that with a mattress.

Chrissie, however, was not asleep.

"Bad, bad, evil, evil." Her fist pounded down again and again onto the teddy bear's crotch.

I stepped back, aghast. I almost yelled at her to stop it. It took a very deep breath. I entered the room slowly.

"Chrissie," I asked softly. "What are you doing?"

"It's a bad place. Got to keep it safe."

"And who is this?" I touched the bear.

"Little girl."

"Are you her mommy?"

Chrissie shook her head. "Mother."

"Did your mommy do this to you?"

She shook her head again. "Mother."

"Oh, Chrissie." I put my arms around her and kissed her hair. "Darling, your mother may have done that to you, but most mothers don't. There's nothing wrong with your body. It's a beautiful body. All of it is. You're a good little girl, Chrissie. A very good little girl."

We sat for several minutes that way until I noticed that Chrissie's breathing was deep and even. I wriggled her around. She was asleep.

I found Bob out in the back yard. He stood gazing at the stars through the trees. In one hand was a small black calf-bound book, in the other, a rosary. His lips moved silently.

I'd seen the little ritual before, and didn't interrupt. It was the one part of Bob's life he kept to himself. Not his religion, just that one prayer time, every evening. He'd stand out in the rain and do it. Happily. It had something to do with connecting to nature. Not all that strange when you consider Bob's made four pilgrimages to Assisi, Italy, and the shrine of St. Francis.

He made the sign of the cross, kissed the crucifix, and opened the book. He tilted it towards the house, so he could see. Not that he needed to. I'm sure he's got it memorized.

As he came in through the sliding glass door, he turned and started.

"For my sins," he muttered, and self consciously fidgeted with the rosary before sliding it into his pocket. He smiled softly at me. "Praying with me?"

I shrugged. I didn't want to admit that I wasn't, and maybe I was. Instead, I told him about what Chrissie had been doing.

"So now what?" he asked.

"Good question." I went into the kitchen.

There was a bottle of merlot on the counter left over from dinner. Bob's godmother is French, and got him on the wine with dinner habit during the summer he spent with her in France. I got wine glasses from the cabinet, and Bob uncorked the wine.

"You know the tough thing is that I feel that Chrissie's mother has every right to teach her what she believes," I said. "I mean the abuse is appalling, but if it's part of their religion. Where do you draw the line?"

"I haven't the faintest." Bob sipped and leaned against the counter. "If I were a fundamentalist, I could probably tell you."

"You were a philosophy major. You should be able to find some answers."

Bob chuckled. "The whole point of philosophy is to raise questions, not necessarily answer them. That's why I also majored in zoology. Our problem centers around the conflict of the basic right to hand down values to one's children, versus the child's welfare, and who has the right to define what the child's welfare is. It's all very well to debate the issue, but when it comes down to applying it practically, who can say? The best answer I can come up with is to find Chrissie's mother, and let her have her say."

"Even if it means talking to people who beat

the crap out of me?" My smile was a bit on the smug side.

"I suppose it does." Bob reached out his hand and squeezed mine. "Where are those copies you made?"

CHAPTER SIX

I have talked to some pretty weird people in my time, including kids who were flying higher than seven forty sevens. But the people that I talked to that next morning buried the needle on the weirdness meter. Most of them were pretty harmless, floating along on platforms of peace and free love, with varying elements of New Age philosophy thrown in for good measure. There were a few that really scared me, including a survivalist group that believed California would be the field of Armageddon.

"Out of all of these, there's only one that sounded like it might be it," I told Bob. "It's called the Temple of the New Jerusalem."

He was taking advantage of the cats still being out to do an extra thorough scrubbing of the cages.

Mango had not been let loose. Bob goosed him along to the cage next to Sweetness's, and scrubbed his, too.

"Is it in Santa Monica?"

"No. It's off Hollywood Boulevard and Western."

"Hm." His mind mulling it over, Bob swept what little water he'd used through the last cage. He's been pretty conservative about his water use since the drought.

"The way I see it, we have two basic problems," he said. He continued pushing the broom over the rest of the patio area. "One, is that the cult where we think Chrissie's mother is? And two, assuming it is, how do we get in to talk to her?"

"And three, what if she's not there?"

Bob grimaced. "Why don't we worry about that when it happens?"

"What if a rival cult kidnapped her mother?" I put on some gloves and got a bale of hay at the other end of the yard.

"Brenner, it's complicated enough." Bob also got on gloves, and a bale of hay, and joined me in spreading it through the cages. "Let's not look for any more trouble than we've got already."

"That reminds me. After we're done with this, I'd better call my machine and get my messages."

I called after lunch, which was late because Bob had to chase the lions out of the hills. The cats were all caged, and the little cats had been kicked out. Janet had called—no one had asked after Chrissie. My temporary agency wanted me to go do books at a cheap outfit that produced commercials, and a lot of headaches for me. I was glad I'd missed it. Bob was paying me to take Laxie out the following Monday, and it was more than I'd make working for those other guys all week. Then Sergeant Griswell called.

I called him right back. I was put on hold for five minutes.

"Miss Finnegan?" Griswell asked when he finally picked up.

"Yes, you called me. What's up?"

"Well, a couple funny things have turned up on that kidnapping you saw. I gave your description of the woman to LAPD missing persons on Tuesday, and they came back with a probable ID, except for one thing."

"What?"

"She's been found."

"What? Where?"

"Well, it's complicated, Miss Finnegan.

The woman you described as being kidnapped fits the description of a Patricia Halford. She's been a missing persons case for four years. The only reason the guys fit the two was that Halford's parents called up Tuesday morning to say that they had recovered her safe and sound."

"So the kidnapped woman can't be Patricia Halford."

"Not necessarily. This morning, some commuters found Halford's body dumped next to the road on the Simi Freeway. The parents have ID'd it, and the dental records make it a cert. The parents also say that they didn't tell the police that their daughter had been recovered."

"Do you know how she died?"

"Word has it she was beaten and her neck was snapped, but that's not official. Given the kidnap angle, LAPD would like you to come down and look at the body as soon as it comes out of autopsy. I doubt it's the same girl, but it can't hurt."

"Probably not. When do we go?"

"Won't be til tomorrow. Will you be at home? I'll have the guy call you."

"I'm at my friend's place. It'll be just as easy to reach me here." I gave him the number and hung up.

Bob had let the dogs loose, and Chrissie was playing with them while he cleaned those cages. I turned purple when Morocco mounted up on Lady. Chrissie didn't seem to notice, and I wasn't about to educate her. Bob noticed and puckered up at me. It's hard to think of Bob as getting horny, but he has his moments.

"Why weren't they doing that yesterday?" I asked.

"Lady just went into season this morning. And let's be honest, Morocco will mount up anywhere he can stick it."

"You're giving me ideas."

"That's my plan." Bob slid up next to me and his lips tickled my ear. "I'm going to get you so horny, you'll agree to anything to get it from me." He licked my earlobe and was gone.

Because of Chrissie, I held off telling Bob about Sergeant Griswell until after she went to bed. That meant over supper. I was a little edgy about her not eating a second night in a row. Bob reminded me that she'd get hungry eventually.

He took advantage of it. That meant candlelight with chicken breasts piccata, his best crystal and china, and a really good chardonay his folks sent him from Napa. His dad teaches at UC Davis, at the vet school there. They frequently send Bob bottles from the neighboring wineries. The china and crystal Bob bought on his last trip to Europe. He'd had a really good year. His sister, Linda, picked it out.

Unfortunately, the setting did not fit the grisly subject at hand.

"What do you make of it?" I asked Bob when I'd finished telling him it all.

He shrugged. "It could mean anything, even that rival cult of yours. In fact, that could explain why someone waited four years to tell the police not to look for Halford. And that's assuming Halford is the woman we saw kidnapped."

"Funny thing, too, Griswell never said one word about a child being missing. Chrissie's six. She would have been two when Halford went into the cult. Why didn't Griswell say anything about her?"

"I was thinking the same thing."

"So it can't be the same woman."

Bob chewed thoughtfully. "Did you tell Griswell that?"

"You know, I didn't." I frowned. "I didn't even think of it. I forgot to tell him about the cult, too. I wish I had. He might have known something. I'd still like to get a look at that body. Just to be sure, you know?"

"It's not my cup of tea. But why not?"

After dinner and clean up, Bob brought the rest of the wine and the glasses into the living room. He put Kiss Me Kate on the stereo, and we snuggled up on the couch. The phone rang. There's a speaker phone on the lamp table.

Bob hit the speaker button. "Hello?"

"Bob, it's Carol." Bob's middle sister. Sue's the oldest girl, and a year younger than Bob, and Linda is the youngest sister. Brian is the youngest in the family. "I've got great news. I'm so excited."

Bob rolled his eyes at me. "So what's up?"

"Why do you sound so far away?"

"I've got the speaker on. What's the news?"

"Testy. Wait. You're not alone."

"Brenner's here."

"Hi, Brenner!"

I rolled my eyes. "Hi, Carol."

"So what's your news, Carol?"

"Oh, that. It's so wonderful. I'm dying, I'm so excited. I'm getting married. Jeff proposed to me."

Bob swallowed. "Congratulations. I'm really happy for you two."

And envious as hell, I was sure of it.

"Mom is having the engagement party on Assumption, the Saturday after, actually. I think it's a Thursday this year."

"It's the height of the TV season."

"That's what Sue said. You guys can just work around it. Oh, and Brenner, you're supposed to go, too. Bob can get someone else to feed his cats."

"Thanks." I was anything but grateful.

"I gotta call Linda. I am so excited."

"Bye."

"Bye."

Bob got up and turned the phone off.

"I'm sorry," I said softly.

Bob sang along with the record. "So taunt me

and hurt me..."

"Bob."

"...deceive me, desert me. I'm yours til I die."

"Bob!"

He poured himself another glass of wine. "Look, I was the one who always wanted to be a priest. And girls were not the reason I left the seminary."

Given the way he kissed me, I was pretty sure boys weren't the reason, either. I felt like shit. Bob heard me sniff and whirled around. He landed on his knees, and put his head in my lap.

"Brenner, don't. It's nothing you can help. Sure, I get frustrated sometimes. I can imagine how badly you must feel."

"Or don't."

"Damn it, cut that out!"

"Cut what out?"

Bob got up and sat next to me. "You put yourself down again. Will you stop it?"

"It's hard. You get into the habit of beating everybody to the punch. At least that way I don't have to listen to people say it."

"What makes you so damn sure people are?"

"I've only been hearing it all my life."

Bob pulled my head onto his shoulder. "I think I'm going to feed your mother to my lions. You just remember I'm not saying it, and I don't want you saying it, and I'm not going to let anybody else say it."

His lips just barely touched mine when the phone rang. Irritated, Bob slapped on the speaker.

"Hello?"

"Hi, Bob. It's Deanna." She sounded more distressed than usual.

"Oh no, is something new going down?"

"I don't think so. How's Mango?"

"He's in great shape. What's with you?"

"Um, Bob, do you know any other tiger handlers in town?"

"A couple. Why?"

"We got a complaint in this morning. Some guy was mistreating a tiger on Beverly Boulevard, of all places. LAPD sent it over, with the guy's license plate."

"Oh, shit. Don't bother reading it. I don't know what they saw, but it was probably me."

"What?"

"Some guys were roughing up Brenner, and Sweetness was in the van, so I got her out. All I did was cue her to snarl."

"Wait," I said suddenly.

"Who's that?" asked Deanna.

"Brenner," said Bob. "I've got my speaker phone on."

"Bob, tell her about the cult," I said. "They may be trying to make trouble for you."

"A cult?" asked Deanna.

"The guys who were roughing up Brenner," said Bob. "We managed to run afoul of some religious fanatics, they followed her, and caught her on Beverly, and I cued Sweetness to scare them off. I was just bluffing."

Deanna laughed. "Bob, you wouldn't sic Sweetness on anybody. You're too worried about her digestion. It was an anonymous tip, anyway. If it's religious weirdos, then I'm not going to worry about it. But I do have to check, you know that."

"I understand. No problem. I'll talk to you later."

He turned the phone off. His lips pressed shut, and he sat, thinking.

"They're harrassing you," I said.

"That's what it looks like. Did you get the license number off that Caprice?"

"It's in the van. Interesting. They'll use the demon government if it suits their purposes."

"These are not nice people. It's too dark to round up the hoof stock. Somehow, I think it's better

60

the cats aren't loose. But I'm going to turn on the fence." He got up.

"Great. There goes the electric bill."

When he came back I could tell he'd been thinking.

"Brenner, we have a problem with tomorrow."

I sat up. "What do you mean?"

"You've got to go look at that body. I want to go with you, partly to back up your ID, and partly because there's safety in numbers. On the other hand, on the off chance that it is Chrissie's mother, I don't know if it's a good idea that she's with us. And on top of all that, I've got that production company of Sue's coming in to dress and preset. I can't cancel the contract, but I don't want any of those cult crazies sneaking in with the crew."

"Bob, do we have any reason to believe the cult knows who you are, let alone where you live?"

He shrugged. "I doubt it. However, they know I have a tiger. It shouldn't be that hard to track me down, especially since I make it fairly easy to get a hold of me."

"And you can't afford to go into hiding, either. Speaking of, have you listened to that song for that video shoot?"

This morning while you were making your phone calls. The production manager brought it by, and I went ahead and signed the contract. I figured we didn't have any trouble last night, it should be okay."

"Well, security is usually pretty tight on a set, especially with name talent around. But what do we do about tomorrow?"

"I'll get Linda to baby sit."

"Can't Sue? She'll be here anyway, won't she?"

"She'll be in and out. I should still call her. Wait." Bob suddenly grinned, and it was positively evil. "I just thought of a way to get around it if the shoot's harassed."

"The video?"

"Them, too. Only I'm not as worried about that. I can blame that on animal activist groups, and everyone gets it from those radicals. I just don't want to blow the ranch as a location. It's saved my ass during more than one slow year."

Bob hit the speaker button on his phone and dialed.

"Hello, Wes. It's Bob," he said when Wes picked up. "How's it going?"

"Well, it's about time we connected."

Bob grimaced. "Damn, I forgot about that."

"No big. The shoot's not til September. It's a feature film. Great little western. You might even like it. I'm pulling the crew together. I want you to head up the animal crew."

"A western? Why do you want me?"

"We've got a stampede scene, and I need somebody with a lot of experience."

"Oh, really." Bob looked at me. Something was up.

There were a lot of other people with better cattle experience than Bob, not that he couldn't have handled it.

"Look, I'll send over the script and you can look it over."

"Don't waste your time, unless it's the one they're shooting."

"Just tell me you'll think about it."

"I'll think about it." Bob rolled his eyes. "Oh, Wes, I nearly forgot. Have you heard anything about Limelight's new episodic?"

"Uh, yeah. It's some sort of modern day ranch soap. ABC is pushing it big time."

"I heard some religious fanatics are trying to shut production down."

I had to snicker.

Wes chuckled. "Probably too much sex for

their pure little minds."

"Well, they'll be shooting on my ranch Monday and Tuesday. If there's going to be trouble, I'll have to call it off. I don't want anything upsetting my cats."

"I'll check around and see what's going on. If there is, the network will be delirious, especially if the media gets a hold of it. All that free publicity."

"Bully for them, as long as my cats don't get upset."

Wes laughed. "We'll keep your kitties happy. Think about that shoot, will you?"

"I said I would. See you later." He hung up.

I grinned. "Sneaky, Bob. Spreading rumors like that."

"It's self-defense at this point. And I told the truth, essentially."

"You should have been a lawyer."

"I was thinking about canon law for a while." He dialed the phone again.

Linda answered right away, but she wasn't happy with Bob's request.

"Why is it everybody pick on Linda?" she complained through the speaker. "Sue had me babysitting her kids all last week because they had colds, and couldn't go to day care, and Alex had a shoot in the studio, so he couldn't keep them. Now Carol wants me to drop everything in the middle of August just because she suckered Jeff into marrying her. And every time you want to go running off, it's Linda, will you feed my cats? Now, you dig up a kid for me. Wake up, gang. I'm in a doctoral program. I'm working year round."

"Fair enough. I'll see if I can fly Brian down."

"Whoa. You want your place trashed? You didn't see what happened to Sue's the last time Brian baby sat. I'll be there by seven tomorrow morning."

Bob laughed silently as he hung up. I could see Linda's point, though. She adores her niece and nephew and Bob's cats. But with Carol living in Las Vegas, and Brian up at the University of San Francisco, Linda is the resident sucker when it comes to baby sitting.

Bob told Sue what was going on, and the rumor he had fed to Wes. Sue was delighted.

"Oh, I hope somebody does start picketing or something. Can you imagine what it will do for the show's ratings when it airs? I'll be working for the next five years."

"Well, just make sure you pass it on that security has to be tight on this one."

"Don't worry about it. Eddie's cool, and he knows how to keep his grips and drivers in line. I'll be there before they arrive just to be sure."

"And no big trucks on the property. Some of that's sensitive land. Have them hand truck everything in. They can keep it in the barn."

"It's in the contract, Bob. We'll take care of it. See you tomorrow."

"All right. Bye."

"Bye."

Bob switched off the speaker.

"Well," I said. "It looks like everything is settled."

Bob wandered into the kitchen, wandered back after a minute, then played with the phone.

"There. The ringers are off. Next call that comes in, the answering machine will take, and we won't know the difference."

"Good." I pulled him onto the couch.

He snuggled in. "I should probably clean up."

"Why?"

"Linda's allergies. All the extra cats running around here drive her wild. So I try to vacuum, wash the drop cloths and keep the small cats confined."

"That's funny. My mom's allergic to cats, too. But if she's so allergic, why does Linda have a cat?"

"She loves them, so she keeps only one short

hair, gets the shots, and lives on antihistamines when she's here."

"Oh."

"I'll clean up in the morning."

We nuzzled and kissed a little. But mostly we held each other against the worries and fears that nagged us. It turned out to be a most comfortable evening.

CHAPTER SEVEN

I have yet to meet a Zebrinski that wasn't blond-haired and blue-eyed, with a disgustingly healthy physique. Every stinking one of them has nice shoulders with little tiny hips. And not a heart attack among them. Shocking, really, when you consider how much red meat they stuff into their faces. Just another example of how there is no justice in this world.

The smell of bacon frying woke me that morning.

Sue arrived at six-thirty, and Linda at seven. I could hear them bickering and chattering as I dressed after my shower. Chrissie was at the living room sliding glass doors, staring at Sweetness again.

"I just can't get over it," said Linda from the kitchen. "You'll have to document this, Bob. Sweetness's behavior is just too bizarre. I wonder if it's related to her captivity, or if there's a parallel in wild life."

I wandered in and headed straight for the coffee machine.

"Whatever happened to the vows of chastity?" sniggered Sue when she saw me.

Bob went on hacking meat. "I never got that far."

"He hasn't with me," I grumbled. "I'm sleeping in the guest bedroom."

"Sue, you've been working in the movie

industry too long," said Linda. "There's bacon in the oven, if you want it, Brenner." She walked over to Bob and muttered to him in mischievous tones.

"Shut up," muttered Bob through his teeth. He smiled at me. "Brenner, will you help me feed the cats?"

Both Sue and Linda watched me like Sweetness watched food.

I finished a sip of coffee, and shrugged.

"I suppose," I said as if I hadn't been there for three days already, as if I was just doing a favor for a friend.

That really fooled Sue and Linda. Luckily for me, a horn sounded out front. Sue got up and stretched.

"It's about time those bastards showed."

Bob quickly washed his hands. "Hold them off until I get Sweetness caged up and the cats fed."

"Is it all right if I show Eddie around while you're doing that? I've got to be down at the other set..." Sue checked her watch. "Damn. Five minutes ago."

"Let me get Sweetness caged." Bob searched for a towel.

"I'll do it." I got up, and threw the towel at him.

Sue picked up the phone and dialed. The horn sounded again. Bob cussed and headed for the front of the house.

Sweetness was not too thrilled about being caged, but she went without testing me. Inside, Chrissie left the window and played with her bear. Bob came out, and we fed the cats. Linda and Chrissie fed the dogs.

Bob reseeded the aviary, and the other caged birds, and left some meat out for the domestic cats, in addition to refilling the dry food feeder.

Linda shook her head when we finally came in.

"Bob, when are you going to stop taking in more animals?" she teased.

Bob just rubbed her head. She swatted at him. Then Sergeant Griswell called and said the county morgue would be waiting for us at eight-thirty. Yeah. Right.

We were going to make it to downtown from Tujunga at eight o'clock in the morning in half an hour? We took Bob's bug and got there at nine.

Deputy Lawson didn't really care. About much of anything. I suppose making a living showing people corpses that might be their loved ones can force you into that kind of shell. As we passed one room, a woman came out sobbing.

"Why my baby? He was such a good boy. Why him?" She was black, and wore a nice flower print dress. Probably had spent a lot of time trying to instill some values in her kid, to protect him from the drugs, and gangs, and hopelessness that ignorance and oppression force on many of the blacks in our society.

The man with her was Reverend Matthews. I knew him fairly well from school. That man busted his ass trying to keep kids out of gangs, one candle of wisdom against a night of ignorance. Like the kids, he was black, born and raised in Watts. But he had found the way out through education, and had returned to lead others out the same way.

I looked at Lawson.

"Gang banger," he murmured.

"You sure?" I growled.

Bob's eyes were closed, and his voice just barely audible. "Please, O God, hear our prayer for that young man. Grant him light, happiness and peace. Let him pass safely through the gates of death and live forever with all your saints."

It was an instinctive reaction for Bob, but it still embarrassed him, so I didn't say anything.

"It really tees me off," I said when Bob had

opened his eyes. "All these kids see is the fast bucks to be had on the basketball courts, and football fields, and on the street corners. And nobody will give them a chance, so of course, they're not going to bother working for anything."

"That's why you're down there, Brenner."

Lawson shrugged. "One less of the bastards to worry about."

I turned on him. "He's still a human being. His mother is still grieving for him. He still had a brain, and a heart and a soul. Don't you realize it's that kind of attitude that turns these kids into gang bangers? Do you honestly think banging heads locking them into jail is going change anything? Those kids need compassion. They need decent facilities, child care centers, libraries, text books, decent salaries so that good teachers can afford to stay down there and teach them."

"Brenner." Bob caught my arm. "You're right, but you're talking to the wrong person."

"I'm sorry." I blinked and sniffed. "I'm just so sick of seeing this shit."

It had all gone right past Lawson anyway. The viewing went well, at any rate. It was nothing I hadn't seen. Bob was a little put off by it. What few corpses he's seen were prettied up funeral ones. Well, there was that one, from the murder we'd witnessed. But he didn't look at the body after it became one.

The body we'd come to look at was Chrissie's mother. Or what we had thought was Chrissie's mother. The morgue attendant who showed us the body was in a talkative mood, and rattled off the autopsy findings.

"Subject, white female, approximately twenty eight years of age. Cause of death was suffocation by a crushed larynx, basically a broken neck." The attendant grinned at us. "Stomach contents were empty. Subject showed signs of previous battering around the vagina in particular, as well as body and limbs, and just prior to death, battering around the face and shoulders. Rope burns. Basically, she was tied down and had the shit kicked out of her."

"Real pleasant," grumbled Bob.

"Other findings, she used to have a drug habit. No pregnancies. Couldn't have. There was tons of scar tissue on her ovaries, probably congenital, or some childhood disease."

"You mean she'd never had a kid?" I asked.

"Basically."

I looked at Bob.

"Can we look at that body again?" he asked.

It was Chrissie's mother, the one who had been kidnapped. It wasn't our brains playing tricks, making us think it was her because it had been suggested to us. We had been thinking it couldn't have been.

But it was. The overbite clinched it.

"Now what?" asked Bob as we left the building.

"How about lunch, and we mull this one over?" I suggested.

"Sounds good. Chinese, Mexican, French, burgers?"

"Edible."

"That's all of the above."

"Depending on the restaurant."

We ended up at Phillipe's, on Alameda. It was packed. I've never been there when it wasn't. The dining rooms were nice and noisy, making it hard to be overheard. I had pork french dip, Bob had the lamb, and a pile of black olives, which he adores. We split potato salad, cole slaw and a piece of cheesecake, and had two Cokes apiece.

"Basically," said Bob. I tittered. He rolled his eyes. "We now have two completely different questions to answer. Who kidnapped and killed Patricia Halford, with the corollary question, was it her kidnappers who killed her?"

70

"It would seem so," I said. "That attendant said she'd been tied down and had the shit kicked out of her."

"Please. Some respect for my lunch. And there's also the second question, since Patricia Halford is not Chrissie's mother, who is? With the corollaries, is that mother a member of the cult we believe Chrissie and Patricia Halford belonged to, and what was Patricia Halford doing with Chrissie in the first place?"

I swallowed a bite of pork. "You know, Bob, I'm really wondering if Chrissie's real mother is at that cult."

"Why?"

"Something about her name. Remember, she kept saying her name was not Apphia, and when she told us to call her Chrissie, she was so adamant about it, as if we'd try to tell her no."

Bob shrugged. "I remember when Sara was four, she went through a phase where she insisted her name was Cathy." Sara is Sue's little girl. "Sue couldn't figure it out for the life of her. Sara didn't know any Cathies. It's still her favorite name. And Sara was adamant about being called Cathy."

"Sara is adamant about everything."

"True. But if Chrissie was trying to separate herself from the cult, she'd have more cause than usual to insist on a different name." Bob's bite of cole slaw slid off his fork onto the sawdust covered floor. He grimaced.

"She's only six. Would she be able to do something that sophisticated?"

"I don't know. Defense mechanisms can be pretty well developed in kids at early age, especially if they've been traumatized. And we know Chrissie has been."

"Dr. Robbins would know. Can I have one of your black olives?"

"Yeah, but I thought you didn't like them."

"I didn't like you at one point."

"You didn't like anybody at that point." He handed me the olive. "Why did you go out with me that first time? It wasn't persistence. I only asked once."

I sighed. "I wanted to be going out with somebody, and you seemed the least repulsive. And you were the only one who asked." I smiled. "But back to Chrissie. The only real connection with anything that we have is the cult. Why don't we visit the Temple of the New Jerusalem? We can find out if Chrissie's real mother is there, and maybe get some hint as to who kidnapped Patricia Halford, and why."

The Temple of the New Jerusalem was housed in a rundown apartment building off Hollywood Boulevard, a few blocks down from Western. It reminded me of the description of Kansas in the book, The Wizard of Oz, all grey, inside and out, including the people. Like many of these buildings, it was two story and built around what had been a swimming pool. It was floored over with cement, but you could still see the rim.

We parked down and across the street, the only place we could find. The Chevy Caprice from two days before was parked on the same side as the temple, about three cars down. The gate into the complex was locked. I rang the bell.

"St. Michael, Archangel, defend us," Bob muttered.

Inside the gate, a column of children, ranging from teen age to about seven, marched along the ground floor apartments, all looking straight ahead, and dressed in the same dismal manner Chrissie had been.

A woman in her forties and dressed in a nice suit came to the gate. She smiled when she saw us.

"May I help you?" she asked.

"We'd like to find out a little about your temple," I told her with a friendly smile.

"Oh, please come in." She admitted us, friendly, receptive, and certain we'd be new converts in minutes. "Have you heard about the call of the prophet?"

"No," said Bob. "We were just curious."

"Well, it has been revealed that these are the last days." She smiled again. Her dark hair was pulled back into a tight bun, but otherwise she looked like any other church person. "Our Savior, Himself, has returned, as He promised he would in the Bible, under the guise of a common laborer named Leland Mattheson. We are the Elect, those chosen before time to be citizens of the New Jerusalem. Those who have answered the prophet's call are coming here to wait until the Savior has gathered the full number foretold in Scripture. Then, together, we shall enter triumphantly into the New Jerusalem, and the rest of the world will perish, according to the Divine Plan."

I tried not to shudder, and I could see Bob biting his tongue.

"Is the Savior here?" I asked.

"Oh, no. He is at the site of our deliverance. This is but an outpost, where we do our best to gather the Elect together."

"Is there a leader here?" asked Bob.

"Of course. Reverend Pastor. Would you like to speak to him?"

"Definitely," said Bob.

"Come this way, and I'll show you some of the Temple and the work we do here."

The classrooms almost made me throw up. The children were taught to read, as long as they read Scripture, and the perversions of it that the "Savior" had written. In all the rooms we saw, guys in the same cheap suits watched, and there were bars on all the windows. The men roamed like guards at a prison, inflicting punishment at whim. Our guide explained that firm discipline was necessary to cleanse the influence of the outside world, as the

Elect must be perfect to enter the New Jerusalem. That meant making the kids behave like robots, and beating them when they didn't.

The nursery was the worst. There had to have been about ten babies in there, and they were all silent.

They had been completely swaddled, so that they couldn't move at all. I know a tight swaddling is supposed to keep a baby feeling secure. These guys had gone beyond tight.

Bob's lips kept getting tighter and tighter. He doesn't get really angry too often because he deals with it in very healthy ways. When he does, it's not a pretty sight. I hadn't seen him hit anybody. Yet.

The Reverend Pastor's office had two more guys in cheap suits, along with a small bookshelf with a few books and a set of shackles, and a huge dark oak desk, intricately carved and littered with papers. The window behind the desk also had bars, but I noted it had a latch on them so they could be opened from the inside in case of a fire. None of the other bars in the place did.

The Reverend Pastor beamed at us, welcoming us into his fold. He was a large man, and unlike the rest of the men, wore his hair fuller and down to his collar, and he had a beard. Very paternal. His suit cost a bundle, or I don't know good wool when I see it. It certainly fit well.

"Welcome to our Temple," he told us grandly.

"And you are?"

"Robert Zebrinski." Bob put out his hand, and it cost him something to do it.

The Pastor opened his arms. "It gives me great pleasure to greet you."

"I wish I could say the same." Bob backed away. "But it's your temple, run it how you like."

"We're here to find out about a Patricia Halford," I said, quickly.

The Pastor took his seat and glowered. "She's

dead."

"Yes, we know. She was kidnapped last Monday night. In the scuffle, a little girl was left behind."

"You're the ones who have Apphia?" he demanded. "You must return her, immediately."

"Wait," I smiled as nicely as I could. "We're trying to be reasonable. We know Patricia Halford was not Apphia's mother."

"This Patricia Halford died four years ago. The woman who arose as a new creation in her place is named Sarai. She was taken from us, as you know, Monday night. We are trying to find her."

I tried again. "Then Sarai was not Apphia's natural mother."

"Of course not. She was barren."

"In any case, I'm going to be in a lot of trouble if I don't speak with Apphia's real mother. If you'll just let me talk with her, I'm sure we can get this whole mess with children's services straightened out."

"We took Apphia in as an orphan, and gave her to Sarai as a comfort in her barrenness." The Pastor got up and moved around the desk. "Sarai is Apphia's real mother, in so far as that makes any difference in these final days. Now, where is Apphia?"

"In a safe place," said Bob. "In the meantime, why the hell are you being so damned obtuse? Can't you see that we're trying to do what's best for this kid?"

"You are obviously not of the Elect. How would you know what is best for her?" The Pastor's meaty hand landed on Bob's shoulder.

His two guards pinned me at the same time, forcing my hands behind my back, and in no gentle way.

I yelped. That snapped it.

"You frigging, son of a bitch!" Bob's fist whipped around.

The Pastor was ready for him. He stopped the punch, then shoved Bob into the office wall. Bob scrambled up, and stopped. The Pastor stood between him and me.

"Get those goons off of her, you bastard." Bob's voice was low and mean, the tone that could back down a lion in mid-charge.

The Pastor wasn't fazed. "Where is the child?"

"What kind of whacko are you?" asked Bob. "Do you honestly think we're going to say?"

The Pastor nodded. I got the back of his guard's hand in my face. My glasses went cockeyed. I barely heard Bob cussing the Pastor out again. He was really angry. So was I. As soon as my head slowed down its spinning, I yanked myself forward, losing my glasses completely in the process.

It startled the guards enough that I got one hand free. I struggled and flailed, and got my hand on the shackles on the bookshelf. One good swing got the guards off of me. I got a better grip on the chain down where it hooked onto the manacles. Swinging it, I grinned.

"I teach in South Central LA," I told them triumphantly. "I know how to use this."

The guards looked at their pastor. One had a nice gash along his forehead, and with the blood trickling into his eyes, I could tell he wasn't too keen on going after me.

"Out of here," I demanded. "All of you." They waited. "Now!"

Whirling away, I started towards the Pastor. He chose not to call my bluff. It's a good thing. I wasn't bluffing. He scrambled out, all but stumbling over his guards. Bob slammed the door shut after them.

"We're trapped," he groaned.

"Nope. There's a fire escape on this window. Push the desk against the door. It'll slow the reinforcements down."

Bob grunted while I took the window out of

its frame.

"Are you sure we can get through those bars?" he gasped as the desk hit the door.

I tossed the screen. "I've been living in apartments for years. Watch this."

It took a little struggling, but the bars popped open. I grabbed the manacles and Bob pushed me out. We both hit the grass running. The gate was between us and the car. Cheap suits tore out from the complex.

"Shit!" I yelped.

We ran the other way. Bob pulled me between two other complexes down the street. He scaled the back fence, then stopped at the top to help me up.

"Fitness training," he gasped, pulling on me. "As soon as we get out of this, you're going into fitness training."

He was braced against the roof of a carport. We scrambled up, and keeping low, ran across it to the next street. Behind us, cheap suits were scaling the fence. We ran like crazy for Hollywood Boulevard.

About four more cheap suits met us there. This time, Bob was ready for them. I took out two with my chain, and fended another off. It sounds really macho, but a chain is a pretty nasty weapon, and it doesn't take much to be effective. A couple quick swings and the guys were down. The leftover was thinking twice. These guys didn't have weapons of their own, nor were they used to fighting people with good street skills.

Bob had taken a couple good hits. He gave three times back. The guy looked like Rocky Balboa at the end of the movie. Up the street were several more cheap suits coming for their turn. Bob pushed the guy he'd pulped at the guy I was fending off, and we headed up Hollywood.

We charged across the street towards an eastbound bus, nearly getting hit in the process. Tires squealed, and it wasn't dubbed in like it is in the movies. I banged on the bus door, and we scrambled on board.

"Go," I told the driver. "I've got my pass in my shorts. And money for him. He needs a transfer."

The driver shook her head and pulled out. I dug my wallet out of my back pocket—I don't carry a purse—and showed the pass, then fished out the buck twenty five for Bob's fare.

"They're just going to follow us again," said Bob as the driver handed him the transfer slip.

"Where's the next southbound bus?" I asked the driver. "And does it connect right away?"

"That be the 206 on Normandie."

"We want to get to Sunset and Wilcox."

"Oh, honey, I'll just drop you at Normandie, you go down a block and catch the twenty three. I'll call ahead and see if he'll wait. But that transfer ain't gonna be no good."

"Terrific," grumbled Bob.

"Here's the stop." I pushed him to the door. "With luck they won't see us get off, and will keep chasing the bus."

"You run for that twenty three," called the driver. "He'll wait."

We ran like hell, but not because we were worried about missing the bus. As we rounded the corner onto Sunset, Bob yelped. He'd seen the blue Caprice turn south onto Normandie from Hollywood.

We were on the bus before they hit Sunset. I could only hope they hadn't seen us get on.

We found a pair of seats on the street side of the bus, and collapsed. The pressure off for the moment, Bob sniffed. There were tears in his eyes, and in mine, too. My nose bled and I tried stopping it with the hem of my t-shirt. Bob put his arms around me, and hung on.

"We're safe," I whispered.

"For how long? We can't stay on this bus forever."

"We're getting off at Sunset and Wilcox. There's bound to be cops around. The Wilcox station is half a block south of there."

Bob let out a sigh of relief. "You okay?"

"Scratches and bruises." I sniffed. "My nose is clearing up. You?"

"The same."

I hesitated. "I hope you're not feeling emasculated by the way I pulled that chain stunt."

"I'm fucking grateful."

"Are you sure?"

Bob grimaced. "Okay. I'm not entirely immune to machismo, and I would have preferred to be the knight in shining armor. But you were closer to the chain. You got a hold of it first. I have to be glad you're not a passive little female waiting to be rescued." He looked at me. "You could have killed them."

I tried to sound flip. "I know."

"Would you have?"

"Probably. You always tell me not to threaten anything I'm not going to follow through on." I waited while Bob thought this over. "Disillusioned?"

"No. I would have done the same. None of us likes facing the beast within ourselves, or in our loved ones."

I squirmed. Bob had to chuckle.

"Hatred you face head on, ready to run rough shod over any who get in your way. But love makes you cower."

"Bob."

"It's true."

I shrugged. "I know what to do about hatred."

CHAPTER EIGHT

This is not to be considered a censure against LA cops. I understand full well the pressures they are under, policing a city the size of Los Angeles, which has a criminal justice system that lets the crooks go almost as fast as they are arrested. When you consider that the jails are bursting at the seams as it is, you can't really blame the system, either. There is a shortage of cops, too, which doesn't help.

Still, some cops are the biggest assholes I've ever met in my life, second only to auto mechanics, or possibly grips, the guys who move stuff around on movie sets. The desk sergeant took ten minutes to come out after the receptionist called him. Just to be fair, I'll assume he was busy. But he had the worst coffee breath I'd smelled in a long time.

"Well, what can I help you with?" he snarled.

Bob had a rapidly blackening eye, torn clothes, scrapes all over his arms, I had scrapes all over my legs and arms, torn clothes, and a huge stain on my t-shirt from my bloody nose. I almost dared the sergeant to guess. I know how futile that strategy is, so I didn't.

"We were assaulted," said Bob. Apparently, he noticed I was going into my attack mode and decided he'd better do the speaking. He's handy that way.

"Do you want to press charges?"

"Actually, we'd like you to send a squad car to

where it happened, and arrest the bozos."

"I'll take a report, if you insist. You're wasting your time, though. Them kids don't stick around after they've jumped somebody."

Bob took a deep breath. "We were assaulted in the pastor's office of the Temple of New Jerusalem. Some of them were young, I'll grant you. But they've got a whole apartment complex of people there. I don't think they're going to be running away."

The desk sergeant's eye fell on my shackles. "Are you sure this wasn't some personal disagreement?"

"We were there trying to find out about the mother of a child we have guardianship of," said Bob, more calmly than I'm sure he felt. "The group insisted we return the child, and when we refused to name her whereabouts, they assaulted us. We picked up the manacles in an effort to defend ourselves. They were in the pastor's office. You might want to ask why they were there, when you investigate."

The sergeant shook his head and looked through the door behind him.

"All my cars are out on calls right now. You're not in any life threatening situation. You'll have to wait until I can bring one in."

I could understand his position. I just wondered why he had to be such a prick about it. We filed a report while we waited. The sergeant was a little testy because we couldn't identify any of the men who actually attacked us. Well, hell, there were six of them, and they all dressed and looked alike. We were a little too busy to look for distinguishing marks. The only person we could nail for certain was the Pastor, and we didn't know his name.

The sergeant did have a squad car drive us up there when the motorcycle cop reported in that there was no one there. By that time, an hour and a half had elapsed since the attack. When we got there, we found the neighbors hadn't noticed the cult leaving.

They'd been too absorbed in the car fire down the street. Guess whose car it was.

"I am really angry," said Bob as we walked through the now empty complex. "I can't believe this. They even got the furniture out."

"They did have a lot of people," I pointed out. "And it was pretty Spartan."

Officer Michaels, who had driven us up, looked around.

"You sure you got the right place?"

I dug into my pocket. "Here's the address."

Michaels shrugged. "This is it."

"Of course it is," said Bob. "They covered the pool up, see? And here's the office."

The door hung open.

"My glasses," I said retrieving them. I bent them back into shape and put them on, then pointed out the several reddish brown spots on the floor just inside the door.

"What do you make of those?" I asked.

Michaels knelt and felt them. "Not yet dry. Okay, it confirms your story. We'll hand it to the detectives and hope for the best."

Michaels was pretty nice about Bob's car, and called the Triple A to get it towed. They arrived promptly, for a change. Not that it would do much good. The Bug was totalled. As if burning weren't enough, the tires had been slashed and the windows smashed. The guys at the body shop offered their condolences and to call a taxi.

"Brenner, what time is it?" Bob asked wearily.

"Quarter til four."

"Shit, we gotta run." He pulled me to the street, and waved back at the body shop. "I'll call you when I figure out what to do with it."

There wasn't a bus due for another fifteen minutes according to the lady on the bench. However, a branch office of Bob's bank was only twelve blocks west down Hollywood Boulevard. We didn't run, but we just barely made it inside.

"What are you doing?" I gasped as Bob got in line.

"I need a new car."

"Oh no, you don't. You need that money to live on. Your electric bill is going to be a fortune."

The next open teller signalled us. Bob pushed past me.

"I need money orders for fifteen thousand," he told her. "Here's my account number. Take it from savings."

"I'll need to get this approved." She didn't seem to think it would be.

"Look, I need to buy a car tonight. I just lost mine, and buses don't go out to Tujunga."

"You could get a ride," I grumbled. "We could even borrow my brother's car. Heaven knows, he never uses it."

"Nope. I'm going to get my Miata." He nodded at the teller, who left the window to do all the bank things she had to do to get the money orders. The manager came by once to check Bob's ID, and they called the branch in Tujunga to fax over a copy of Bob's signature card so they could compare it.

While we waited, Bob looked over at me a little guiltily.

"Brenner, I know it's hard for you to understand. It's just something I've gotta do. Knock me down once, I bounce back bigger and better."

I didn't say anything. What could I say? Instead, I reached out and held him. It had been a shitty afternoon. The two of us sniffled and blinked and wept and held each other. It must have looked pretty ridiculous, two bruised and bloodstained people hugging and crying in an almost empty bank, while the employees glowered at us because they wanted to go home.

We took a bus to the nearest Mazda dealer. I couldn't help nagging him a little.

"We should be comparison shopping, getting quotes, finding out exactly what options you want, and how to get the best price on them."

"I don't want any options. Everything I want comes standard, or I can install it cheaper myself." Bob smiled at me and patted my hand. "I've test driven it five times, too. Believe it or not, Brenner, I've actually put some thought into this."

I have to admit, Bob knew exactly what he wanted. And he did not beat around the bush at all, which startled the salesman. He looked at two or three, looked in the window of an electric blue one, double checked the sticker, and then collared the nearest guy. It wasn't as easy as you might think. For some reason, the sales people were avoiding us.

"Nice evening," said the lucky man with a weak grin. He looked us over, then pretended he didn't see what a mess we were. "How are you folks tonight?"

"I want to buy this car," said Bob, showing him an envelope. "I've got the money orders. What kind of discount will you give me?"

"Well, uh... Why don't we step into the showroom and discuss this."

"I don't want to talk. I just want to buy the car and get out of here."

"Great. Fine. Um, step this way. I'm Monty Seidler.

You are?"

"Robert Zebrinski. Nice to meet you. I want this specific car."

"Right. Let me get the number off of it. Great. Um.

This way, please. Is this Mrs. Zebrinski?" He smiled at me.

We spoke at the same time.

"Girlfriend."

"We're friends."

I had never bought a car with cash before.

They offered us coffee and tea. They showed Bob a discount. I looked over his shoulder.

"What about that other dealer?" I said quickly before Bob could accept. "They gave us a better figure."

Mr. Seidler let out a nervous laugh. "Better than that?"

We looked. I looked at Bob. He looked at me. Mr. Seidler looked at us. This was definitely getting harder than he thought it would be. I picked up a pencil and wrote down another figure. Mr. Seidler looked at it.

"You've got to be kidding."

"That's what the other dealer offered us," I said. "He was a bit of an ass, which is why we're here. But I'd rather save the money, wouldn't you, Bob?"

"Certainly. You want to take off?" He got up.

"Uh, why don't I check this out with my manager," said Mr. Seidler. "Have a seat. Would you like some more coffee?"

"None for me, thanks. Brenner?"

"No, thank you."

Ah, the joys of follow through. Bob wasn't exactly thrilled, because if we left that meant another long bus trip. But he had to give me credit when Mr. Seidler came back with the paper work. Of course, by the time we added on the tax and license, the money orders were pretty well played out. Oh well. We drove out of there, after putting the top down, of course.

At the first stop light, Bob leaned back. Peals of laughter erupted from him.

"Are you all right?" I asked, giggling a little.

"You're an old Yankee horse trader, aren't you?"

He reached over and hugged me hard. "Oh, Brenner, I'm so glad I've got you!"

He kissed me hard, too. The light turned green.

We didn't notice until we got honked at. Bob

waved, slipped the little car into gear, and away we zipped.

CHAPTER NINE

We stopped for dinner at a restaurant in a strip center at Crescent Heights and Sunset. As we lingered over Chianti and pizza, I frowned.

"Problem?" Bob asked.

"I haven't checked my messages all day," I said.

He shrugged. "There's a pay phone outside. Why don't you check them while I pay up?"

"Have you got the money?"

"For a change, I—" Bob stopped and checked his wallet. "Yeah."

I dialed, waited through my announcement, then pushed my code number.

"You have three messages," the machine's voice told me.

Beep. "Brenda, it's Janet. Call me. Now."

"Shit," I muttered while the machine told me she'd called Friday at 11 a.m.

Beep. "Brenda, it's your mother." She sounded more agitated than usual. "Uh, honey, something strange is going on. Would you call me as soon as possible? I'll talk to you later. Bye."

"Friday, 4:15 p.m."

Beep. "Brenda, Janet here. I've really got to talk to you, kiddo." She sniffed. "I just hope you're all right. Please call me. I'm at home."

I hung up without resetting the machine.

"What's wrong?" asked Bob, coming up.

"I don't know." I dialed Janet's home number. "Janet called twice. She was mad the first time, and upset the second."

"Hello?" asked Janet's voice.

"Janet, it's Brenda. Are you okay? What's wrong?"

"Thank God. Is the little girl all right?"

"She's fine. She's with Bob's sister."

"How about you?"

"I'm fine. What's wrong?"

"You better get over here. Is Bob with you?"

"Yes."

"Him, too. I can't explain over the phone."

"We'll be there within a half hour."

I had to direct Bob. Janet lives in Cheviot Hills, a ritzy neighborhood just south of Century City. Her husband is a plastic surgeon, which is why Janet can afford to be idealistic. Janet didn't look so good when she opened the door. Her eyes were black, and her lip was swollen.

"What happened to you?" I gasped.

"What happened to you?" Janet asked. She let us in. "You two look like you've been through a meat grinder."

"It's kind of a long story, Janet. Why don't you tell us what happened to you first?"

Janet sighed and showed us to the living room.

It's all white, with soft white upholstery on the two couches. Janet also owns two dogs, three cats and a parakeet, none of which are white. She also has two kids. Very idealistic.

"It's been one hell of a shitty day," she grumbled. We all sat down together. "It started this morning. Those guys in the suits were back, watching me. Apparently, they harassed some secretary into giving them my name. Then the other office wanted to talk to me. A Florence Woodfield had called in asking about the Jane Doe. When she found out you had her, Brenda, she hit the ceiling, swearing she was going to file a complaint, didn't we check our people, why did we let that girl go home with someone who owns a tiger? Which is exactly what my supervisor asked me, since I'm the one who vouched for your character."

"I don't own a tiger," I said simply.

"That's what I told my supervisor. I also told her that I had been to your apartment, and if you had a tiger in there, then I was a blind woman. She bought it, and wrote Woodfield off. Later, however, I remembered you told me that Bob is an animal trainer, but that you didn't mention what kind of animals he trains." She glared at both of us.

"I told you he specializes in cats."

Janet picked up the long hair at her feet. "I thought you meant Fluffy. Not Tony the Tiger."

"Mrs. Levy, my cats are well under control," said Bob. "Chrissie doesn't go anywhere near them. If I have to take them out of their cages, she stays in the house."

"Oh great, you've had her out there."

"I was there, too," I said. "Bob's never been alone with her, so your puritan tight asses can stuff it. How did you get those shiners?"

"Those." Janet shivered and sniffed. "When I left work, those suited guys came up to me and insisted I knew where... Apphia was the name, where she was. I told them I did, and said if they were her legal guardians, I'd show them where they could get her released to their custody. Big help that was. They said I was to bring them to her. I said we had to fill out the paper work first. Then they got rough. They also said to tell you that they knew where you and your lover were, and that you would be next."

"Holy shit," I groaned.

"There's nothing holy about it," said Bob.

"I would have laughed in their faces about the lover part, if I could have." Janet sniffed again.

"It looks like you two met up with them after all."

"They're a religious cult," explained Bob.

Together, we told Janet the whole, incredible story.

"Oh, my god," she groaned when we finished.

"What are we going to do about this?"

"Nothing," said Bob. "Chrissie is safe, certainly safer than she'd be with that cult. We've got the police looking for them. You don't just move a hundred plus people without someone noticing. As for who Chrissie's mother really is, God only knows at this point."

"True," agreed Janet. "And that cult may yet have legal custody. Tell you what. I'll go through the adoption records for the past five years. I know Halford was only with them for four, but you never know. If the cult has custody, we'll be on their doorstep investigating. Even if they don't. Geez, the abuses you were describing. The only other problem is what to do with Chrissie."

"She's fine with us," said Bob a little defensively.

"It's not going to last," said Janet.

"Why not?" I asked. "She's happy. She starts with Dr. Marshall the end of next week. I'm keeping everything kosher with her and Bob."

"But what about the cats?" Janet asked. "Bob, it's not you. I'm sure you're perfectly careful. But you both know I have a bureaucracy to answer to. If something happened to that little girl, and accidents are always possible, we'd never hear the end of it."

"She'd stand a better chance of running into the street and getting hit by a car," said Bob, his voice getting tight.

Janet nodded. "She would, and I don't blame you for being angry. It's the same thing as with the single male problem. These people have their little blinders on. All they see is what the regulations say, and they say a safe environment. You are probably

90

providing that. But the bosses frown on dogs, let alone lions, tigers and bears."

"Just to set the record straight, I don't have any bears," said Bob. "And I only have one tiger."

"Any lions?"

"Two."

"Anything else?"

"A cougar and a lynx, three border collies, a host of small birds, two parrots, a toucan, a cockatoo, several domestic cats, two horses and about sixty head of sheep and cattle. I also have a variety of rattlesnakes, rabbits and raccoons on the property, but I don't provide for their welfare, so I don't count them."

Janet closed her mouth. "How do you take care of all that?"

"They're my living. I work them all. Except the wild stock. The rattlesnakes, by the way, are all in the hills. They don't come near the house. And I've already seen to it that Chrissie has heavy boots."

"It's work, Janet," I added. "But I've helped out at times, and it's not that bad."

She sighed. "Well, I will feign ignorance. Part of my revenge against the tight asses. But, Bob, Brenda, someone will find out about all this, and Chrissie will not be able to stay with you."

It was depressing. Lucky for us, we had more bad news waiting for us when we got back to the ranch.

"This friend of yours, Bob," said Linda. "Wes?"

"Yeah."

"Well, he called today. He said he was hoping you'd take the job, and he had just thrown some business your way. He gave directions to the ranch to some guys who had called looking for you. They wanted to come up and look at the tiger. Wes told them about the other cats."

"What time did he call?"

"Around five thirty."

"Shit."

"It gets better. These guys in goofy looking suits, you know, super nerds? They started hanging around about an hour after that until the security men guarding the location trucks shooed them off. And for the royal tee off, Sweetness and the rest of the cats were having fits all the time they were here."

"I don't need this," said Bob.

I had just hung up the phone from a talk with my mother.

"Like you need this, too," I told him. "Mom says these guys in bad suits are hanging around her place. Apparently two days ago, someone called up asking if my mom knew a Brenda Finnegan, and she said yes, she's my daughter. Now Mom wants to know all about this kid I supposedly have. Where did she come from? Why do I have her? For God's sake, don't give her to the weirdos in the suits."

"As if you would," grumbled Bob. "Terrific. It sounds like they went through the Finnegans in the phone book asking for you."

"Or my relatives. Mom said today they started hassling her, and when the police got there, they disappeared. She's scared, and she can't keep calling the police, because they just leave and the police can't stay there all the time, and she can't afford a bodyguard. They told her she should have somebody move in with her."

"Why not one of your brothers?" asked Bob. I have two, both younger, and no sisters.

"Eric already lives with her."

"Is he being hassled?"

"He's never around."

Sighing, Bob looked at Linda. "You know, Linda, maybe you'd better stay here tonight. I'll sleep on the couch. You can have my bed. Brenner, do you mind sharing a bed with your mother?"

"You don't want her to stay here, do you?"

"I don't know what else to do. These clowns

have already beaten up your best friend. See if your mom can call the cops out long enough to get in her car and get away from there."

I had to do it. It took Mom two hours to get up there from Long Beach. I fidgeted the whole time, and apologized to Bob at least every five minutes for bad-mouthing my mother so much to him. He'd never met my mom. I'd been avoiding it. Bob hadn't really asked to, either. Given how neurotic I am, he figured it came from someplace.

It isn't my mother's fault that she's so critical. You should hear my grandmother go after her. And Grandpa was an alcoholic. So if all these books on adult children of alcoholics are true, it's no wonder my mother's a mess, or that I am.

Mom buzzed from the gate around ten o'clock. I felt my guts twist worse than when... Well, worse than they had in a long time.

"It's okay," I told myself as I paced. "Bob and I are just friends. It's no big deal. I can have friends. It doesn't have to be romantic."

Linda looked at me strangely. "I thought you and Bob were going together."

"For heaven's sakes, don't give her that idea!" I snapped.

"Linda, cool it," said Bob.

I heard the car park. "I'll go out and get her."

I turned on the porch light and went out the front.

Mom stood next to her car, wrinkling her nose. I'm so used to it, I don't notice it anymore, but with all those animals, Bob's place doesn't exactly smell like a rose garden.

"Am I parked in the right place?" Mom asked.

"Sure." I looked over at the drive. The gate was firmly shut, and no one was about. "Whatever you do, don't touch the fence. It's electrified, and Bob's keeping it on to keep those guys out."

Mom looked at the ten foot tall chain link

with the rows of barbed wire on top.

"I guess that's reassuring. Brenda, what does this guy do for living that he has to keep an electric fence like that?"

Jubi roared in answer. Mom jumped and screeched.

"Mom! Hush. You'll upset them."

"That sounded like a lion, and awful close, too."

"That's what Bob does for a living that he needs the fence."

Jubi roared again, and the others snarled and growled in response.

"Bob's a studio animal trainer for movies and TV," I said, picking up her suitcase.

Mom followed me to the house. "You mean he keeps lions here?"

"He keeps several big cats. They're all in cages." I opened the door. "Welcome to Fort Zebrinski. Mom, this is Bob and his sister, Linda."

"How do you do, Mrs. Finnegan?" Bob asked. He shook her hand, then took the suitcase.

"It's Doris, please. Nice to meet you, Bob, Linda."

"You, too," said Linda.

"I'll put this in the guest room," said Bob.

"Come on in," said Linda. "Would you like something to drink?"

"Ice water, thank you."

Linda went off to the kitchen. Mom grabbed my elbow.

"He's not living with her, is he?" she asked softly.

"She's his sister," I hissed. "She's here for the same reason you are."

"How did you get messed up in this?"

So I told her how, the Reader's Digest version without all the violence. Mom shook her head.

"Brenda, you always did bite off more than

you could chew."

Bob ambled in. "Well, you're all settled in."

Linda came in with a glass and coaster. "Here you are. Well. Isn't this crazy."

"Yes." Mom settled into the couch. "Bob, Brenda tells me you train lions for the movies."

"And a few other cats." He went to the window and turned on the outside lights. "Take a look. They're active now." He pointed them out. "That's Sweetness on the end. She's a Bengal tiger."

"Sweetness?" Mom got up.

"She is just the most lovable kitty," said Linda.

"Next to her is Mango. He's a cougar. Someone was trying to make money showing him off. The cat next to him is a female African lion, her name is Eudora. We rescued her and her mom from this traveling circus. They were grossly mistreated. Her mom passed away a couple years ago."

"That's too bad," said Mom.

"Her mate is Jubi, as in jubilate. He's next to her."

"A real king of the beasts, isn't he?"

"He likes to think so. Next to him is Laxie, the lynx."

"He seems awful small."

"Lynxes don't get that big."

"They're beautiful."

"They'll take your face off if you don't know how to handle them." Bob grinned wickedly.

Mom backpedalled. "You have such interesting pets."

"They're not just pets. They're my living. And they can be dangerous, so please don't go outside without telling me."

"Certainly. I'll be glad to."

I sighed. "The sad part is, those guys in the suits are far more dangerous than any cat could ever be."

"It takes a human to build a nuclear bomb," said Linda.

Mom's smile was a little strained. She went to clean up shortly after. I got out the linens for the sofa.

Linda decided she might as well go to bed, too, and went.

"Brenda, have you got any toothpaste?" Mom wandered out from the back.

"Yeah. It's in my bag on the back of the toilet."

"That's yours."

"I sometimes spend the night, okay?"

"Fine. Why are you being so testy?"

"Nothing, Mom." I stuffed a pillow into the pillow case.

"Is Linda sleeping out here?"

"No. Bob is. She's sleeping in his bed. I'm sleeping with you."

"Oh." She wandered over to the sliding glass door and squinted outside. "What's he doing out there?"

"Mom!" I turned. "He's just praying. Don't bother him."

"I wasn't going to." She looked at me as if she were about to say something. "Let's go to bed."

"In a minute, Mom." I concentrated on making up the sofa.

Bob wandered in just as I finished.

"How are you doing?" he asked.

"Fine."

"Let me guess." He knew I wasn't going to tell him. "You're feeling as if every nerve ending in your body is exposed and being rubbed raw."

"I'm all right."

"Brenner." He took my shoulders and massaged them.

"I shouldn't let her get to me. And she's not that bad."

"Will you please? Deal with what you're

feeling, and quit trying to justify why you shouldn't."

"Bob, she can probably hear everything we're saying."

He looked into the hall. "The door's shut. Come here."

He pulled me onto the couch.

I had to giggle. "Taking me to your bed at last."

"For the moment." He nuzzled my neck. "Look, I understand. Your mother is not the Wicked Witch of the West. But every time you get around her, you end up strung up tighter than a high tension wire. So deal with the fact that her criticism hurts you to the bone, and let it go."

"Wonderful." I blinked. "I love that line. Let it go. It's so fucking easy to say, and nobody ever tells you how."

Bob's fingers rubbed my temples. "Just relax. Think about breathing. In and out. In and out. Now, pretend that all the tension in your body, and all the hurt is a big wave, and visualize it in your mind's eye, flowing out of you. There it goes, flowing out of the tips of your fingers, and out of your toes. Do you see it?"

"I see a sine wave. Sine of x for zero less than or equal to x less than or equal to two pi."

Bob laughed. "All right. You do seem more relaxed, so I'll let you get away with it this time."

"Thanks. I do love her, Bob."

"I know. That's why she can hurt you so badly." He put my head down on his shoulder.

"It's not her fault. My grandmother is not known for her sweet disposition."

"And that's not your grandmother's fault, or her mother's fault. You can trace these things all the way back to Eve. It's not going to do you any good. All you can do is stop the cycle when you have your own."

"Assuming I do. I never wanted to have kids because I was always afraid I'd visit worse on them.

Daughter becomes mother, trashing yet another daughter."

"Brenner, that won't necessarily—"

"Bob, I just thought of something." I sat up.

"Now, don't change the subject."

"About Chrissie. When she was beating up on her teddy bear. I asked her if her mommy did that to her. She said no, Mother did."

"We know Patricia Halford was not her mother."

"That's not it. Mommy's the good guy. She wants her mommy. She remembers her real mother."

Bob thought it over. "Okay."

"Now, remember that Reverend Pastor said that she was an orphan, taken into adoption. We only have his word for it that she's an orphan, and dollars will get you doughnuts, she was taken. Literally."

"You mean kidnapped?"

"Stolen."

Bob sat back. "That's not at all unlikely. All right. We've got two objectives now. One is to find that cult and put them out of commission long enough to get them off our backs, and two is to find Chrissie's real parents."

"What about Patricia Halford's kidnappers, slash, killers?"

"Objective number three. We'll have to put that one on hold, though, until we get the New Jerusalem out of our hair."

I mused. "You know, they're looking for her, too."

"That's what's really disgusting about them. We could be working together, pooling our resources."

"Well, Bob, what do you expect? Look at how they close themselves off from everything, and turn their brains to mush."

"Indeed." Bob reached over and nuzzled my ear.

I got up. "I gotta get to bed."

I kissed him and hurried into the back.

Mom was in bed reading when I slid under the covers next to her.

"What took you so long?" she asked.

"Bob and I were going over strategies."

She sneezed, and reached for the tissues on the bedside table.

"You okay?" I asked.

"Just my allergies. Must be all the dust, and I smelled hay, too." She rolled onto her back. "Brenda, Bob seems like a very nice young man."

"He is."

"He's not gay, is he?"

"Mother!" Bob's kisses burned on my lips once more. Bob was not gay.

"It just seems strange. He's, what, thirty, and he's never been married, and you're just friends."

"Mom, the man has morals. That's all. I know it's a little strange for this day and age. But that's the way he is."

"All right. I'm sorry I asked." She rolled away.

"Mom, I love you."

"I love you, too, honey."

I rolled onto my side and closed my eyes. I hate it when my mother does things like that. It wasn't true, but like always, she managed to plant that seed of doubt.

I pushed it from my mind. At worst, Bob was bisexual. Even then, he just wasn't the type to get it wherever he could. He sure wanted it from me, though.

"It's my plan," his voice whispered in my mind. "I'm going to get you so horny, you'll agree to anything to get it from me."

Why not? Women have been doing that to men for centuries.

CHAPTER TEN

I got up at six thirty the next morning, not because I wanted to, but because I wasn't about to face my mother without a good, stiff fix of caffeine. I bumped into Bob in the hall.

"You look like hell," I grumbled. He did, too, with his hair on end, beard growing, and his eyes swollen shut. "Bad night?"

"Haven't had my coffee yet. Can I get into the bathroom?"

After a cup apiece, he began to look a lot better. Even his black eye didn't look so bad.

He held up the pot. "More juice for the battery?"

I nodded, and he poured one for each of us. He was at least able to formulate words. I hadn't gotten that far.

By the end of the second cup, we were eating toast and clear-eyed.

"Nothing like a coffee jump start," said Bob.

Linda staggered in, and he pressed a cup into her hands.

"Fuck, I hate mornings," she grumbled.

So did Bob. In fact, we had that in common. We both hated getting up early but had to.

He went out to get the cat pans. I looked in the refrigerator and concluded that someone was going to have to go get some groceries if we were going to eat until the siege lifted.

"Let's see, we've got five eggs," I mumbled. "And leftover chicken, and some salad greens."

Linda, still comatose, ignored me. I went over to the pantry.

"Oh, good. Oatmeal."

"Oh, yuck," muttered Linda.

"Oatmeal?" asked Chrissie, who had wandered in.

She was freshly bathed and dressed, and I knew damn well my mother was still asleep.

"You want some?" I asked.

Chrissie nodded.

"You clean up all by yourself?"

Chrissie nodded. She got out the cereal bowl and looked at me expectantly. I made oatmeal.

As soon as the water was on to boil, I beat the eggs together and chopped up chicken and celery. Bob came in with the pans and grimaced.

"Oatmeal?" he asked.

"If you don't like the stuff, why do you have it?" I asked.

Bob thought. "Everybody has oatmeal. I don't know anybody who eats it, but everybody has it."

"Well, that's all there is beside five small eggs and some leftover chicken. We've got to do some serious shopping."

"The tomatoes are ripe." Bob looked at the wall chart depicting his vegetable garden. "The beans should be coming in, and there's spinach, and the lettuce patch. I've got ham in the freezer, and we can always cut steaks off the cat food. If worst comes to absolute worst, I can butcher a cow."

"There is no bread. You're assuming the raccoons haven't gotten to the garden, and we could use some eggs and milk, and fruit."

"You and I have also got some errands to run. Fine. I'll call the Sheriff's department. Maybe we can get a squad car to ride by here at regular intervals."

The Sheriff's department was glad to help. I

guess they figure Bob's cats keep crime down in the neighborhood.

I kept the oatmeal warm, and held off on the eggs until my mother got up. Bob started in on the meat for the cats. Linda suggested baking our bread, but there was no yeast, so I made biscuits instead. Linda took over on the kneading when my mother came in. She, too, staggered for the coffee machine. Chrissie slipped out of her chair and into the living room.

"How is everybody this morning?" Mom asked.

"Fine." Bob slammed the cleaver down on a particularly tough joint. Mom jumped.

"Cat food," explained Linda.

"Want some oatmeal, Mom?"

"Thanks."

I got out bowls and plates and silverware, the everyday stuff. Mom gave me a hug.

"Such a busy helper, Brenda. You've always been so good at that."

"Thanks, Mom." I put the frying pan on the burner and prepared to dump the eggs in.

"Honey, heat your pan first. And don't you need to grease it?"

"It's nonstick, Mom." I turned the burner on.

"May I have some milk for my oatmeal?"

"We're out."

"What's Chrissie going to drink? My god, Brenda, she has to have milk."

"We'll be going to the store later," said Bob, hacking with more vigor than usual.

"All right." Mom clearly wasn't happy about it.

"Brenner, if you're done with those eggs, can you help me with the cats?" asked Bob.

"Sure. Linda, can you help with the dogs?"

"I'm already on it." Linda scurried outside.

"I'll finish cooking," volunteered Mom. She

stirred the eggs, chicken and celery together and took it all off the flame.

Linda came back in with the dog pans and looked into the living room.

"Hey, Doris," she called. "Come look. You've gotta see this."

Mom looked and yelped. "What in heaven's name?"

I looked at Bob. Chrissie and Sweetness were staring again.

"They like each other," said Linda.

"You sure that tiger's not thinking lunch?"

Bob laughed. "Not Sweetness. Game playing maybe. Brenner, will you get her caged up?"

Mom turned white. "Brenda, you're not going out there, are you?"

"Mom, I know how to handle her. Bob's a good teacher."

"Well, for God's sake, be careful!"

I rolled my eyes at Bob and went out. Right. I was going out there to get Sweetness to charge me. She didn't. But she got stubborn. I had to physically yank her from the sliding glass doors. My mother nearly had a heart attack.

"Come on, you stupid cereal mascot." Tugging all the way, I got her into her cage.

Sweetness snarled. Not a serious one, just mildly perturbed, as if to remind me that Tony was a male and a cartoon, at that. I shut the door and she shook her head at me.

"You don't even think about giving me trouble, cat," I told her. "I'm in a bad enough mood."

Sweetness snorted and yowled, then curled up in the back of her cage to sulk.

Linda came out with the dog food. Bob joined us and fed and petted Mango.

"Why don't we check the garden after this?" he suggested, then looked back at the house. "I want to talk to you."

"I'll go get the log."

I went into the kitchen. Mom sat alone, finishing breakfast.

"All done?" she asked.

"Yeah."

"Brenda."

I stopped. I knew that tone. It usually preceded a fight.

"Yeah, Mom."

"I'm a little worried about having Chrissie here with those cats."

"Bob has been working those cats for a lot of years. He knows what they can do, and, believe me, he's not going to let Chrissie near them."

"He lets you."

"He's been teaching me."

"He's certainly big-hearted." Mom got up and brought her dishes to the sink. "I wonder if he isn't too much so. One person can only handle so many animals."

"Mom—"

Bob opened the door. "Brenner—"

"I'll be out in a minute, Bob."

He glanced at my mother, then me. "I'll be out in the garden."

"And why doesn't he call you by your name?" Mom demanded as soon as the door was shut.

"It's a nick name, Mother. It's no big deal. Will you butt out?"

"I'm not butting in. I don't know how you can say that."

"Then what's with the third degree with the cats, and Chrissie, and how many animals Bob has?"

"I am merely concerned. Brenda, you have obviously been seeing this man for some time."

"We're good friends." I went over the drawer under the wall chart and got out the log book.

"And I am your mother. I have a right to know what is going on in your life."

104

"Why? So you can tell me everything I'm doing wrong with it?" I slammed the door shut.

"That's not fair."

"Then why are you picking on me?"

"I'm not picking on you. I ask a few reasonable questions, and you fly off the handle." She was using her reasonable tone, too, the one she used when she was being anything but.

"And you're not worried sick because I'm seeing a guy who likes lions."

"I am not worried, Brenda. Yes, I'm concerned. You close me out of your life. I have to chase you down every time you move. Why can't you talk to me?"

"You want to know why not? Because you find fault with everything I do."

She looked hurt. "Now, darling, you're exaggerating."

"Oh. You weren't up five minutes before you told me how to heat up the pan. And shouldn't I grease it first? Didn't it occur to you that maybe I knew it was nonstick? You tell me how to dress, how to fix my hair, how to fucking brush my teeth."

"You don't have to swear."

"And you say I'm exaggerating."

"Brenda, honey, I don't know where you get these crazy ideas. I'm only trying to help you. Darling, you're such a beautiful, wonderful person. I want other people to see it."

"That's not the way to do it, Mom," I yelled.

"Then what am I supposed to do?" she snapped. "Let you run around looking like a bull dyke, being just friends with some man who raises dangerous animals, and won't even call you by your name?"

"Yeah, Mom. That's exactly what you're supposed to do."

"That is ridiculous!" She gaped as if she couldn't believe what she was hearing, although it was nothing she hadn't heard before.

"Well, did it ever occur that maybe it's none of your damned business?"

"You are my daughter. It is my business."

"I'm over twenty one, in case you hadn't noticed. I'm capable of making my own decisions. If you don't like that, it's too fucking bad. And if you say one more word against my friend, who had the decency to ask you here because he was worried about your safety, then you can fucking get out and face those assholes from the cult by yourself!"

I slammed the door as I ran out. Why Bob was still on the patio was beyond me. I did see Linda inside out of the corner of my eye. She was laughing. I ran past Bob, straight to the garden. He was there less than a minute later, his arms around me. I sobbed onto his shoulder.

"Fight?" he asked softly.

I nodded. "Not a real bad one. Damn her. She always makes so much sense, and she's dead wrong."

I told him everything that we'd said, even the part about him. Bob didn't say anything. He just listened. I'd never told him everything before. It felt good.

We picked tomatoes and salad greens. The beans wouldn't be ready for another week. The small cats had kept the raccoons and birds away, and a combination of lady bugs, praying mantises and beer, kept most of the insects away.

Right before we went back in, Bob hugged me and kissed me so softly and lovingly, I began to feel as if my mother didn't matter.

Mom was still in the kitchen. Linda was there also.

They'd been talking. I wasn't about to ask. But Mom looked at Bob as though she really liked him.

The first order of business was to get groceries in.

Linda had something up her sleeve when she suggested that she and I go to the market. Bob didn't seem to know what it was, and was less interested in finding out. The list took some haggling, but after it was done, Bob figured that between his own supplies and what we bought, we could wait the summer if that cult didn't let up. Of course, working would be a problem. But it was only Saturday. We'd worry about that on Monday.

In the supermarket, Linda chattered almost constantly. In fact, I'm not sure what she was talking about when she suddenly laughed and grimaced.

"Bob never could do any wrong."

It was the first sour note I'd ever heard from Bob's family.

"I don't get it." I looked at the rows of canned beans. "Did he say black beans or pintos?"

"Here's the list." Linda handed it to me. "What don't you get?"

"What you said about Bob doing no wrong. You almost sounded bitter."

Linda laughed. "Not bitter. It's just ironic, is all. Everybody is always so amazed that Bob's so secure. It's not surprising. In our house, life revolved around Bob. My parents really tried, and they did love us all equally. It's just that Bob was Mom's favorite, and we all knew it. I think the reason that I'm not screwed up is that Mom made a point of being close with each of us. She lets us tease her about it, too. She tries not to be, but she's besotted with the turkey."

"You're the first person I've met who's called him that."

"I lived with him most of my life. I can afford to realistic. And poor Brian, my god. He's lived all his life in the shadow of Saint Bob. Dad has busted his butt trying to remember that they're two different people. It hasn't always worked."

"I can't imagine your family fighting with

107

each other."

We're allowed to be honest about how we feel, which is the one thing that saved us. And there are times when Bob behaves like a holier than thou jerk, and we've always been able to call him on it. We take turns ganging up on each other. That's the one nice thing about being from a large family. There's always somebody to take your side."

"You all seem so much alike."

"We all look alike. I used get called by my sister's names all the time. In fact, a few years ago, before Dad went to Davis, someone thought Brian was Bob. He was so PO'd." Linda suddenly hugged me. "I think this is why I wanted to come out with you. It's funny. Your mom is a lot like mine, only my mom admitted it when she was bitchy, and from what she told me, your mom's had a lot rougher life. She's really proud of you."

"I know. It's just a different dynamic. Your family found the healthy way to deal with these things. Mine didn't."

"It's not the end of the world. I mean, I remember when I first met you, you were so standoffish. Dad thought it was hysterical."

"Why?"

"He says Mom was just the same way when he met her." Linda giggled.

My heart stopped. "Oh, shit. Does Bob know this?"

"No. What's the problem?"

"Just don't tell him, will you?"

"Why not?"

"Cause it'll get his hopes up. Linda, he wants to get married, and he knows I don't. It really bugged him when Carol called about the engagement."

"Oh. Okay."

Linda's quiet capitulation bothered me. It was as if it didn't matter. Perhaps it didn't. I remained on edge for the rest of the trip.

108

We had taken Bob's Miata, with the top up. As we drove up the hill towards the ranch, Linda frowned.

"There's that blue Chevy again."

I checked the mirror. "Damn. It's them. That's their car."

"They didn't follow us."

I had to laugh. "It's the new car. They can't see us turn into the ranch from where they're at."

"Thanks be for the sheriff's department. I wonder if my place is under siege."

"My mom's house still is. She called my brother at work, and he said they were still there. He's sleeping over with friends."

"Did he get hassled?"

"He got home too late last night, and when they asked him about me this morning, he said Brenda who? He'd gotten Mom's note by that point."

While we put groceries away, Linda called her friends. The cult guys were staked out at her apartment. Bob called Sue just to be sure, but since she went by her husband's name, she hadn't been bothered. I called my brother Brent at his bookstore. He hadn't been bothered, either. His home phone is unlisted, and the bookstore is called Bookland. No way to connect a Finnegan to it, unless you knew to look.

CHAPTER ELEVEN

"I don't understand," I told Bob as we took off in the Miata again. "Why talk to the Halfords if we know that Patricia was not Chrissie's mother?"

"Because I want to verify everything Reverend Pastor told us. They may yet know something."

That was always possible. Bob had gotten the names of Patricia Halford's parents from her obituary in the paper, and the address from the phone book. He'd also called ahead, so they knew we were coming.

Mr. and Mrs. Raymond Halford lived in Pacific Pallisades, north of Santa Monica, in a ranch style house nestled into a hillside of lush greenery. Mr. Halford was resting, Mrs. Halford told us as she let us in.

"His blood pressure bothers him," she said. "The doctor recommended naps to help him relax."

She looked comfortable, in an expensive pale pink sweat top and pants. Her hair was short and frosted to cover the gray. She wore tinted rimless glasses with large hexagonal lenses.

We sat down in the living room, which was furnished in expensive colonial, Ethan Allan as opposed to Sears. The whole house looked as though it came straight out of a magazine layout.

"You seem at peace," Bob said cautiously.

Her smile was sad. "I am, in a way. Patty's finally at rest. These past four years have been difficult. It was Raymond who kept hoping, searching.

Trying all the detective agencies, and then the Reverend. Poor thing. She was our most difficult child. The rebel. I wonder now if we were too hard on her. The other two turned out all right. Maybe not. We just found out last month our other daughter is getting a divorce, and our son's oldest is in therapy. Raymond insists they indulge the child too much."

"Seen and not heard?" asked Bob.

Mrs. Halford nodded. "And spare the rod, spoil the child. We spanked all three of them. None of them turned out violent. Patty turned to drugs. She always told her father he never understood her. Poor thing. I don't think she ever understood herself. We did everything for her. She finally came around. Started going back to church. Talked about getting married and having a baby. She really wanted a baby. Was desperate for one. Even talked about artificial insemination, and raising one by herself. Raymond hit the roof. Two days later, she disappeared."

"Did any other children near you disappear at the same time?" I asked. "Around two, three years old?"

"Oh no. All our neighbors around here are like us. All their children grown. We have a few young families at church. Thank God, none of them have had to go through what we went through."

"Thank God," added Bob. "Did you have any reason to suspect that she joined a religious cult?"

Mrs. Halford nodded. "We always wondered about that. The police now seem to think so. We never had any idea one way or the other. I take that back.

She did say some funny things the night before she left. Something about Christ's return. That set Raymond off again. He said if Christ had returned, he would know about it. We're Christian, you know. Raymond leads a bible study. He's been doing it for years. We believe very firmly that the Bible is the word of God. Patty disappeared so completely. I tried to hope. But something in my heart knew I'd never see her again. I think God was trying to prepare me."

"Do you know if your husband called the police to tell them that you had recovered your daughter?" I asked.

"No, of course not. I haven't the faintest idea who did." Mrs. Halford frowned. "The police also asked about a little girl. We knew nothing about one. It's all very confusing, especially how Patty came to be found off the freeway. Raymond wanted to hire a detective to find out who killed her, but I asked him not to. I believe it's not for us to know. Let her rest. I hope I've answered your questions, Mr. Zebrinski."

Bob nodded. "About as many as you can." He looked at me.

"I don't have any more questions."

We got up.

"I hope I've been able to help your research. I suppose you can't talk about the related matter."

Bob grimaced. "It's ticklish. It concerns the little girl I told you about."

"Oh. I do hope you find her parents. I'll be praying for you."

We thanked her and left.

"All right," I said. "Halford is as in the dark as anyone can get."

We got in the car. Bob had put the top down as soon as we had gotten away from the ranch. The blue Caprice hadn't budged, and never seemed to notice us, and I watched them as we went past when we left. I don't know what they were looking for, but I was thankful it wasn't a blue Miata.

"I wish we could have talked to Mr. Halford, too," said Bob starting the engine. "But I've got a feeling he couldn't have told us anything different. What time is it?"

"Three thirty. Why?"

"Good. We've just got time to do another hip hop down to Marina Del Rey, and talk to Dr. Chritener."

"Who's he?"

"An expert on religious cults, and on debriefing their members."

"Hm."

Dr. Chritener's townhouse overlooked the Marina. Obviously, there was a lot of money to be made debriefing cult members. He met with us wearing an open shirt, shorts and Birkenstock sandals.

"Okay, let's get down to brass tacks," he said as we got settled in his living room. "You want to know about the Temple of the New Jerusalem because you've come into guardianship of a child that was with them."

"Not to mention the fact that they are harrassing the hell out of us," I said.

"They're good at that," said Chritener with a toothy smile. "They have no problems with using physical violence to get what they want. The good news is, they don't use weapons beyond a club, or a rod. The bad news, they are damned persistent."

"Who are they?"

"It was started about twelve years ago by Leland Mattheson, a diagnosed schizophrenic whose family left him a very big fortune. Commitment proceedings got bogged down in the money issue, and believe me, his relatives would have done it if the man were completely sane, so there was some justification for the defense."

"But Mattheson was really insane," said Bob.

"Is. He's still around. Talk about your delusions of grandeur. If he was going to develop a fantasy persona for himself, he made sure he went straight to the top. Went around claiming that he was Jesus Christ, here for the second coming. He built a core of followers with the help of James Ready, an otherwise ne'er-do-well type, known mostly as a drifter and a two-bit con man. No one knows for sure if Ready really believes Mattheson, or if he's just landed one hell of a good con. I tend to believe the former. Money collection is not a major issue with this group, although the higher ups live pretty damned well."

"We noticed," I said.

"They also tend to recruit among the down and out." Chritener shrugged. "It could be Ready's just a hell of a lot more subtle than people give him credit for. It's not all that important a distinction, really. The scary part about these guys is the strict control. Everyone is completely regimented, and everyone's task is to bring in as many of the Elect, the fourteen thousand or so that will make it to heaven according to Revelations, that they can. That's fourteen thousand men, by the way. Apparently each guy can bring along as many women as he wants."

"So very generous," said Bob. "What about the sexual abuse?"

Chritener giggled. "Now, we're getting weird. Sex is supposed to be irrelevant. It's the Last Days, there's a set number of people who will get in. Why bother? The women beat up each other's vaginas as a sort of purification, especially after every menstruation. They start in on the girls almost as soon as they are born. They aren't supposed to like sex, and the guys make sure they don't. Coupling is quick, ritualized, and the guys get in line for it."

I gasped. "You mean several men in a row will…"

"Essentially gang rape the woman." Chritener nodded. "For some reason the men haven't figured out, there aren't a lot of women in this group. The ratio is roughly two point eight men per woman. They do know it's easier to get the women in if they let their women do the talking, which is why a lot of them are on the streets. They are kept under guard, however. The guys hang back and keep an eye on things just in case. Kids will sometimes go along to make it all more friendly and normal looking."

114

"They're big on purification from what we've seen," I said.

"Oh, yeah. They must be cleansed and made perfect, usually through ritualized battery. They're not a fun group, and they do some significant ego damage. That's one of the reasons down-and-outers are such good candidates for them. Their egos are already in the gutter. Even with the beating, being part of the Elect makes them something."

"Why do they engage in sex, and have women around if it doesn't make any difference?" asked Bob.

Chritener sighed. "The best I can figure is that the end is due soon. So what they can't convert, they'll breed. They're a medium sized group, not more than a thousand members. And they need fourteen thousand males. The women are basically baby machines. They get to be among the Elect because they need the babies. Mattheson is not all that young a man."

What about the way they got out of that building so fast?" Bob asked.

Chritener laughed. "They've had to make tracks before, my man. They're good at it. The main group is housed on Mattheson's farm near Fresno. The locals have no complaints about them, at least nothing to serve a warrant on. It's Mattheson's own land, so getting them off would not be easy. The minor temples, there are about three of them, are scattered around LA, and they do tend to move about. I'm surprised the number in the phone book was good."

"It had been changed, now that I think about it," I said.

Chritener nodded. "As far as getting rid of them, good luck. You seem to have the right strategy. They don't want trouble with local law enforcement. The one ray of hope, you will get Sundays off. They're all in their temples then. They also avoid harrassing people at their places of employment because that brings in a lot of notoriety, and more law enforcement.

115

As far as the little girl is concerned, I personally recommend no debriefing. It's a dirty business, and the way you described her over the phone, she wants to distance herself from it, which is seventy percent of the battle right there. Just keep her with a good psychologist."

"You don't use violence, do you?" I asked.

"Only to defend myself." Chritener chuckled. "Debriefing is a real ticklish process. You can do a lot of damage to someone whose brain has already been turned to oatmeal. Then there's the personal rights issues, which are important, but the results aren't always that healthy." He shrugged. "Given what I've seen a lot of these cults do to people, I'll take my chances with the ACLU." His eyes suddenly bore into us. "I hope you two weren't planning on doing any debriefing."

"Absolutely not," said Bob. "I know when I'm in too deep, and I don't mind admitting it."

"Me, too," I said.

Chritener nodded. "Had to be sure. Amateurs are a real problem. They often make it all ten times worse. I've worked with kids that had to be institutionalized thanks to amateurs. This is not a job for someone without the proper training and experience."

We chatted a little more about other cults, and things of that nature and left. A car from the Sheriff's department was just pulling past as we started up the hill to the ranch. The Caprice had moved elsewhere. I smiled, feeling relaxed and somewhat optimistic.

Fights with my mother tend to clear the air between us for a while. Between that and what Bob and I had learned from Dr. Critener, I was of the opinion that I could survive another few days with my mother, as long as she wasn't around that Sunday.

Dinner changed my mind.

She didn't say anything. I could see her biting her tongue, though, and that was worse. I had no idea what I was doing that bugged her, and began to fantasize worse offenses than what probably upset her.

Bob, fortunately, saved me the trouble of asking him to get rid of her for a while, and invited her to ride with him, Linda and Chrissie to round up the stock so he could let a couple cats loose. I offered to clean up, to let them get out there earlier.

As soon as they were gone, I called my brother, Brent. He was not enthusiastic. Actually, he's not enthusiastic about anything, being a notorious plodder. Say he was more disinterested than usual.

"It'll be really awkward," he complained.

"Like it's not awkward here? Come on, Brent." Too late, I heard the kitchen door open. "She's got me completely stressed out. My boyfriend is ready to shoot her."

"Boyfriend?" Brent was bemused by the revelation, and reacted as if I had mentioned a hangnail in passing. "Oh. I didn't know you were seeing anybody."

Or something like that. I wasn't really listening.

Bob was the one who had opened the door, and grinned at me triumphantly. I flushed and turned my back on him.

"It's no big deal. We're more friends than anything. In any case, you know how Mom gets. It's your turn to put up with her for a while."

"You been seeing this guy long?"

"A while. What about Mom?"

"A while, huh. That's cool. Why don't Margie and I have you over for dinner real soon?"

"Margie?" The light dawned "You're living with someone, aren't you?"

"Didn't I tell you Margie moved in?"

"You didn't tell me Margie existed. Wait. Is

she that writer?"

"Uh huh."

"And you didn't tell Mom she moved in."

"Well, you know Mom."

"Why do you think I'm trying to dump her on you?"

"You're living with Bob?"

"No! She's just driving me nuts. Look, Brent, I'm going to tell her that it will be easier for her to get to work if she stays with you. You'll see her tomorrow. Bye."

"Okay. Bye."

How much of that sunk in, I have no idea. I told Mom later that night that Brent had invited her. If Brent disagreed, Mom probably assumed he'd forgotten that he had. Brent is like that.

Then there was Bob. He was still rooting around in a drawer for something I'd give even odds was already in his pocket.

"You called me the b-word." His eyes twinkled innocently.

"It was the easiest thing to say."

He "found" what he wanted, and straightened.

"Your Freudian slip is showing," he said and left.

"Fuckhead," I muttered.

CHAPTER TWELVE

Sunday was indeed a day of rest. Linda took off early because she was scheduled to read at mass at her church that morning. She wouldn't be back because she was going to a conference in San Diego starting Tuesday, and decided she could squeeze an extra night's stay out of her friend. Mom took off pretty quickly, saying she preferred to go to her church, and she'd be at Brent's that night in case Eric called.

Bob fed the cats before he showered and with only his jeans on so he could get to mass on time. He's a Eucharistic Minister there, and was scheduled to serve. Since we've been seeing each other, I go because I feel guilty when I don't, and it's all his fault.

The first reading was from Jeremiah. "Woe to the shepherds who mislead and scatter the flock of my pasture, says the Lord." I have to admit, I felt pretty smug thinking about that cult, and Leland Mattheson. Until the homily.

Father Matt is pretty cool, and usually makes you want to do better without bogging you down with the weight of your sins. He had to talk about our responsibility as Catholics to live as examples to the rest of the world. To be open and tolerant of other people's ideas, and loving. I kept thinking about my chain. At the Temple of New Jerusalem. Real loving, beaning those guys like that.

After mass, Bob damned near shook me.

"You were fighting for your life," he said when we got back to the house.

Chrissie was back in the living room, staring at Sweetness again. She hadn't liked mass too much, but she didn't misbehave. I almost wished she had.

The indoor cats had been let out of Bob's room and wandered about.

"I know." I fumbled with the plates as we set the table for lunch. "But seriously, Bob. What makes us so damned sure we're right?"

"What do you mean?"

"How do we know that what we believe is the truth? What if Leland Mattheson really is the second coming?"

"He's not." Bob stopped as what I had asked sunk in. "I don't know. You look for the inconsistencies, the hypocracies."

"There isn't a religion in the world that doesn't have some of both." I shooed Rambo off the table.

"Perhaps in the people. But I haven't found too many in the doctrine itself. But then, I've studied it. I don't know, Brenner. I guess it isn't ours to know. That's why it's called faith."

"Then do we have a right to say that the Temple of New Jerusalem is wrong?"

Bob came over and put both of his hands on my shoulders.

"Brenner, I can't answer that. There are an awful lot of people in this world who can open their bibles and say without a doubt that New Jerusalem's members are going straight to hell. No problem. But they have divorced themselves from the reality that life is not black and white.

"They go to their bible studies. They let their leaders spoon feed them truth without ever thinking about what it is. It's work to think, Brenner. That's why their values are so easily threatened by stupid TV shows, and movies like 'The Last Tempation of

Christ'. It's frustrating as hell. You and I, we spend a lot of time wrestling with our consciences. Does that automatically make us better? Does that make us right? I can't tell you. All I know is that I see people trampling all over our constitutional rights picketing video stores because they don't want their kids damaged by pornographic videos, yet waving those same constitutional rights like a flag if we even hint at taking away their guns.

"I see people bad-mouthing Catholics because we pray to statues and that's idolatry, and yet they want to lock up people who burn flags because it's a sacred symbol. They want to make abortion illegal, and won't vote in taxes for child care centers and prenatal care. Then I look at you, risking your neck down in South Central trying to give some hope to kids who have none. You believe in the flag. You don't support abortion, or pornography. But you choose not to answer those problems with censorship and intolerance. Instead, you spend three days raising hell with public agencies to get a place to stay and health care and an education for a pregnant girl who was going to get an abortion because her mother would kick her out if she didn't. You saved a baby, and the kid has a chance to get out of the poverty and ignorance that got her pregnant in the first place.

"Do we have the right to say that New Jerusalem is wrong? I don't know. I do know that they are cruel, and that they physically hurt their own people. I know that their way of settling grievances is to hurt us and the people we love until they get their way. I know we have a six year old child in our custody who has lived most of her life in fear and pain, waiting for people to hit her.

"Is that wrong? I don't know. All I can do is what I believe to be right, and that is keeping Chrissie with us, giving her love and psychological therapy, and using the resources of the legal system to keep New Jerusalem from hurting our loved ones. And whatever we can do to find Chrissie's birth mother and the persons who killed her adoptive mother. Sure, I could condemn them, but what good will that do? And in the final analysis, that's what has to be considered. It's work, but it's the only way we can know we are right."

I fidgeted with a napkin. "That's fine for you, Bob. But how many times have you been wrong?"

"Plenty. Just like you. But we've both been right plenty of times, and other times we've been somewhere in between. We can't change any of it. We can just keep going forward."

I let him hold me. From his arms, going forward didn't seem so bad. But his arms couldn't take me into the classroom in South Central, or out on the streets where violence waited to happen, or through nights alone with my fears. And they certainly couldn't bring me to face myself. There are some places we can only go by ourselves. Still, his arms were a wonderful place to rest.

There was also lunch to fix, and an afternoon and evening to get through. We spent most of the time with Chrissie, playing with her, cuddling her. She still wouldn't say much of anything. And she still remained wary and unsure. There wasn't much to be done about that.

That night as I kissed her and tucked her in, she gazed at me.

"Sing?" she asked.

"Would you like me to sing to you?"

She nodded. So I sang. It was pretty grim. My voice isn't that good. And I hate "Rock A Bye, Baby". I don't know how kids survive that image of a baby and cradle falling out of a tree. So I sang the song "Evergreen", the one Streisand sang in "A Star Is Born". It's about love. Well, Chrissie liked it.

Monday morning, the guys from New Jerusalem were back in place. The arrival of the movie crew helped keep them at bay. In the meantime, I had to put Laxie in Bob's van, and take off myself. The blue Caprice followed me until I ditched it in the morning traffic.

It's getting pretty sad when you go to a movie set to relax. The production manager, Jim Donahue, wasn't particularly thrilled to see me. He'd been expecting Bob, and wasn't quite ready to believe that I could handle the job. The director was thrilled. He thought he could bully me into putting Laxie through stunts that Bob wouldn't let the lynx do. Both guys were wrong. Once I established myself, things went smoothly. Well, as smoothly as they ever do.

At the ranch things did not go so smoothly, but it had nothing to do with the cult. The actors were pricks, and stupid to boot. The director couldn't get it through his head that Bob was not going to let the crew herd his cattle with four wheel drive trucks because it would trash the land, not to mention the potential for hurting the calves. Then one of the grips teased Morroco, the border collie, and got bit.

That night, Bob told me the only decent part of his day was hearing me tell how well Laxie did. Tuesday was more of the same. Well, not quite the same.

Jim Donahue, the production manager, sauntered up near the end of the afternoon.

"The office gave me a message for you," he said. "It's from your boyfriend."

I bristled. "We're just friends. What's the message?"

"If you can ditch your excess baggage long enough, he'd like you to swing by Target and get some sandwich containers and Ziplock bags. They're on sale." Donahue smirked. "Sounds pretty domestic."

"It's for his bean crop."

It was a pretty domestic type request. I did it, but then I can't stand to see good food go to waste, and there were a lot of beans that year. Bob uses the bags and plastic containers to freeze the excess produce.

The film crew at Bob's place had left by the time I got there. I left Laxie in the van until I was sure the other cats were locked up and Chrissie was inside.

She wasn't. She sat in front of Sweetness's cage, the both of them staring as usual.

Bob had the dogs loose. He had just finished cleaning their kennels when I arrived. Three short whistles, and the dogs were tucked away. Bob told Chrissie it was time to go inside. She refused to budge. Bob physically pulled her to her feet. Sweetness growled at him, a mean growl.

I swallowed. "Bob, she's never done that before, not to you. Not to anybody, unless you cued her to."

Bob got Chrissie inside. "Yes, she has." He shut the kitchen door and gazed at the tiger thoughtfully. "Not to me. The feature shoot last June."

It was actually last May and last June, and Bob had copped almost a year's salary on that one, plus a minuscule percentage. From the gross. Talk to the accountants on Batman, the Movie, about what a difference that makes.

"I don't get it."

"I told you about it. Angie's husband came to the set for a surprise."

Angie is Angela Jackson, that really soulful nurse, cum artist on Save the Children. You know, the show about the children's hospital. She was the star of the feature, along with Sweetness, and the two really bonded.

"Merritt grabbed her," Bob continued, "and Sweetness snarled at him. Tigers are very territorial."

"Yeah, but about people?"

Bob shrugged. "Sweetness is. You should have seen her last Wednesday, when those cult guys were trying to beat up you. She almost lunged."

"I'd better get Laxie in."

Inside the house, after we caged up Laxie, things got worse. Bob told Chrissie to come to dinner, and she refused.

"Fine," he told her, although it wasn't. "It's time for bed."

"I hate you!" Chrissie screamed. "I hate you! I hate you!"

And she would not stop screaming it. I think Bob knew intellectually that she was just working out anger that had probably been pent up against the cult and their abuse. But it hurt him. He stared at her.

I stepped in. "I know you're angry, Chrissie. That's okay. But we don't say hurtful things just because we're angry. We say we're angry. Now, you can stand in the corner."

Gently, I pushed her to the first empty corner, and stood over her. She didn't stop screaming. Finally, I pressed a pillow into her hands, and told her to tell it how much she hated it. It's a good thing for that pillow that six year olds aren't that strong.

Chrissie eventually calmed down, and crawled into Bob's lap. Gingerly, he gave her a second chance to come to the table. Chrissie nodded, but half a minute later, she was asleep.

"She wasn't yelling at you," I told him as we laid her down on the air mattress.

Bob tenderly laid the sleeping bag over her. "Oh, I know that. It just shocked me."

"And it hurt."

We left the room. "Yeah. It did. I was surprised.

I'm so glad you were around."

"She could have done it to me just as easily." I headed quickly for the kitchen. "And you would have done just what I did."

And I would have been a complete mass of gelatin afterwards, but I wasn't going to share that.

Besides, Bob already knew it.

Bob pulled dinner from the oven and refrigerator.

The table was already set. He shot water at Rambo and Sanders. Sir Toby sat in an empty chair and dared us to make him move.

"That film crew must have left really early," I said, looking it over.

"No. They didn't wrap til four thirty." Bob dished up Beef Florentine casserole. "The strike crew couldn't get here til after seven. I told them to leave it til tomorrow, first thing. And they didn't need me to wrangle after lunch, so I got things done."

"I wonder if those guys from the cult have given up waiting for me at my apartment," I said after grace.

Bob, stung, looked at me. "What happened today?"

"Nothing. Everything went fine."

"Then why are you talking about going back to your apartment?"

"I never said that."

"You were wondering whether our friends from the cult were still staking you out."

"We really need to get some firm strategies together to get rid of them. I'd like to make some attempt to find Chrissie's birth mother, and it'll be that much harder if I have to keep ditching guys in cheap suits every time I turn around. Maybe if we got some more background information on Mattheson, we could trigger an investigation."

Bob sighed. "Brenner, what's gotten into you? You've gone distant on me again."

"No, I haven't. You know, I just had an idea how we might trace Chrissie's mom. One of those missing child foundations, the ones that put pictures of kids on milk cartons. They keep all kinds of records. Chrissie might be listed with one of them."

"Fine." Bob wasn't going to push whatever

it was that was bugging him. He knows me better than that.

That doesn't mean he was happy about it.

CHAPTER THIRTEEN

I spent the next morning on the phone. I got appointments with two missing children groups, a lunch date with Janet, and my messages. My temporary agencies had each called. I ignored them. I had enough work to do. Nolan Casey, from the LA. County District Attorney's office called.

The name and address he left suprised me. The light colored Mercedes that had borne away Patricia Halford belonged to a Reverend Alfred Oakes, and the address, once I looked it up in the Thomas Guide, was in the hilly part of Brentwood, but not anywhere near a certain estate on Bundy. It's still a big money neighborhood. A minister? Either he owned a TV station or his flock was pretty generous with their tithes. Possibly both.

Bob, still moody from the night before, declined to go with me to investigate.

"There's Chrissie, for one thing," he explained testily.

"I thought she could come with us. It might be a good idea for the missing child people."

Bob shook his head. "I've got stuff to do here. I want to work Sweetness before that shoot tomorrow. And I'd like to work with Rambo."

He was making excuses, especially since we both knew Rambo refused to be trained. I got the feeling Bob wanted me to talk him out of it. He should have known better than that. I was enjoying

my freedom. Sort of. I asked for a ride down to the
bus stop, and he told me to take the Miata.

I don't know how we get into these
manipulation games. We both hate them, but once
you're in, it's impossible to get out without falling
into the other's trap.

Janet did not have good news for me. She
didn't have bad news, either, really. Nor was it
unexpected.

"I drew a blank," she said then bit into a huge
corned beef sandwich.

We were in the deli in the Los Angeles City
Mall.

It's a dingy place with cafeteria style service,
and filled with executives and higher up civil
servants. The sandwiches are good and huge, which
is probably why. I had decided to hell with my hips
and arteries, and worked my way around a salami
and provolone on a French roll.

"You mean on the adoption records?" I asked.

"Yep. Three days I spent working on this. We
had Shabbas on Saturday, and I was at temple all
day. But I let myself into the office on Sunday, then
called in sick Monday and Tuesday. If Chrissie was
adopted, it wasn't legally."

"I'm not surprised. We're beginning to think
Chrissie was kidnapped. We talked to Patricia
Halford's mother, and she didn't know anything
about a kid."

"That's an idea. Have you talked to missing
persons?"

"I'm meeting with a couple national groups
this aft."

"Great." Janet peered at me thoughtfully.
"How's Bob?"

I shrugged. "Fine. Got any ideas on what else
we can do?"

"Brenda!" Janet groaned.

"What?" I complained defensively.

"What is going on? Are you and Bob having a fight, or something?"

"What is with you two? Bob's all asking me the same thing last night. Nothing is going on."

"I find that a little hard to believe. I've mentioned him three times today, and each time you've changed the subject."

"So I don't talk about him. What's the BFD?"

"Is he getting too close?"

I swallowed. "No. He's just sulking, okay? I mentioned the guys at my apartment last night, and he thinks I want to go back there."

Janet's smirked. "Well, do you?"

"Of course I do. I'm paying rent on it. I'd like to be able to sleep there."

"While a bunch of violent jerks in cheap suits are waiting to pound you into hamburger? Brenda, what are you running away from?"

I squirmed. "I'm not running away from anything. I'm still at Bob's, if you insist on knowing."

"You are so defensive right now. Was it something Bob said?"

"He hasn't said anything. All right? It's just domestic stuff. I feel like I'm too involved in his life. I have no right to be there. He needs space." I took a big bite of sandwich.

"Not as much as you're giving him. Geez, Brenda, what is it with you and commitments? There are guys in singles bars more willing to settle down."

"I have no problems with commitments," I grumbled around the food in my mouth.

Janet ticked off her points on her fingers. "You move at least once a year, sometimes twice. You've been steady dating the same guy for two years and you won't even call him your boyfriend. You've got a problem, woman."

"It's not commitments. It's intimacy, or so sayeth the shrink. Who cares what it is. I just need to be on my own. I'm happier that way."

No. Janet wasn't convinced. Neither was I, for that matter. At least she had the decency to drop it. It wouldn't drop me. My neuroses have a nasty habit of haunting me long after I've tried to wriggle out of facing them. Or even after I face them. I don't know where people get the idea that I'm lonely. My neuroses keep me in plenty of company.

Each of the ladies that I spoke to at the missing childrens places were happy to see me. They don't run into too many people with children looking for parents. Neither were much help. These things take time, I suppose.

It was getting very close to three when I left the last office. Oh, goody. I had the choice of confronting the minister about his car, or a long, slow, hot drive to Tujunga which would only get worse as it got closer to five.

I called information for Reverend Oakes' number, called it, and got his wife, who thought I was looking for directions to the bible study that night. I told her I wasn't. She gave them to me anyway. I declined politely, explaining that I had a little girl staying with me and no babysitter. She said to bring the girl, and my friend, and anybody else I could think of. I silently mulled over inviting some of my more recalcitrant students, assuming of course they weren't doing time somewhere, thanked her and hung up.

I hate LA traffic. It's one of the reasons I put up with the MTA. In the Miata, the drive to the freeway was murder. Bob thinks manual transmissions are fun, even in traffic jams. I think manual transmissions are a fucking nuisance, and sheer misery in stop and crawl traffic. We both think air conditioners are superfluous in a convertible. I rethought that position all the way to Tujunga. Preserving the ozone layer won, but by a very narrow margin.

I'll leave you to guess what kind of mood I

was in by the time I got to Bob's. His was no less foul. Chrissie had been giving him trouble all day. Then when she was doing time out in the guest room, Sweetness started acting up.

"They're besotted with each other," Bob complained. "Sweetness doesn't want to cooperate unless Chrissie's around. I don't want to give in to bad behavior, but that damned cat is getting out and out touchy."

"You don't want to mess around with that," I sighed.

Bob looked at me for a second, then half smiled.

"Higher purpose," he muttered. "What did you uncover?"

"Lots of nothing except an invitation to a bible study tonight."

"One of us will have to stay with Chrissie."

My grin was tight. "I tried that. Chrissie can come, too."

I glanced over at her. She was in front of Sweetness's cage. Those two were besotted. Bob pulled Chrissie in for dinner. Sweetness yowled sadly and went to the back of her cage to sulk.

Chrissie definitely had a capacity for loud, prolonged screaming. She demonstrated it again as we tried to put her in the van without Sweetness. Sweetness, for her part, had somehow got wind of the fact that we were taking Chrissie, and raised bloody hell.

That upset the rest of the cats, not to mention the dogs, and the birds. Even the horses were fussing down in their stable. Bob was ready to tear his hair out.

"She's got to work tomorrow, with a frigging rock star," Bob groaned.

"You'll have to sedate her," I said.

Bob will not sedate his cats unless they need it for medical reasons.

"I know I am going to regret this, but I'll give in," he said. "Let's get Sweetness in the van."

It was night and day. The other cats settled down immediately. Sweetness purred and thrummed and chuff-chuffed. Chrissie almost smiled. We probably should have left the two of them at the ranch, and only one of us gone to the study. But both of us really wanted to see if the Mercedes was the same one I'd seen.

Bob parked on the street, next to the driveway. The study was not at the Oakes' home. It was next door. Neither house had a car in its driveway. We were greeted by Mrs. Oakes, and sent to the living room. The couples there were mostly our age, and had children with them. Chrissie clung to us.

"And what do you, Bob?" asked a slight young man whose nametag said Will.

"I'm an animal trainer," Bob replied, hedging, although less for the fun of it. Something about the patent leather smiles said these people would not be terribly open minded.

"Really. Say, we've got a puppy we're having a problem with. He's a nice little thing, but we can't seem to housebreak him. I paddle him when he goes on the carpet, but then he goes right back and does it again."

"Try putting him outside right after he eats," said Bob, his smile stiff. He doesn't believe in hitting animals, except in self-defense. He's never had to. "And praise him with lots of petting when he does his thing where he's supposed to. And get the carpets cleaned. He can smell his accidents, and thinks it's okay."

"No kidding. Any hints on getting him to walk on a leash?"

"It depends on how old he is. But I don't really do obedience. I mostly work animals for the movies. In fact, I can't stay too late tonight. We've got a shoot tomorrow."

"Really?" asked a rotund woman with expensive clothes not quite hiding it. Her name was Jill. "That is so exciting. We took the kids to Universal Studios, and they just loved the animal show. It's amazing what they get those animals to do. Are you working there tomorrow?"

"No. We're on location." Bob smiled again.

"My niece is here from Wisconsin, and she is dying to see a real set. She says Universal is mostly hype."

"It is," agreed Bob.

"The guide had to tell her something about going on location, and Sandy has not stopped bugging us, but how do you find out where they're shooting?"

"You go up to the Film Commission office in Hollywood," said Will. "They list everybody who's got a permit, and they all have to have permits. It tells everything they're going to be doing. That's how we know where to picket."

"Are you with an animal rights group?" Bob asked.

"Are you kidding?" Will grinned. "They have their priorities completely skewed. Scripture makes it plain. We were given mastery over the earth."

"Right." Bob held me back from letting the lunkhead know that mastery also meant stewardship, and it didn't mean a license to pollute and destroy God's creation. Bob's a little better at the diplomacy thing.

Reverend Oakes also helped by calling the study to order. He stood before a fireplace decorated with a pump action shotgun, a nondescript man in polo shirt and khaki slacks, with grey temples and half glasses over which his eyes searched the people gathered around him. His voice was good old Southern Baptist orator deep, without the Southern accent.

To say the man was conservative would be understating the fact. Ronald Reagan was more liberal. I think the only difference between Oakes and the Reverend Pastor of the New Jerusalem was that Oakes didn't think Christ had come yet. And I don't think Oakes believed in beating on women's vaginas. Even odds, the only way he knew how to find one was in the dark.

I will give him credit for stating his case well. He found all sorts of bible verses to back up his belief that Care Bears, Smurfs and My Little Pony were going to lead our children straight to hell. GI Joe was okay. He wouldn't even say Ninja Turtles. Glancing back at the kids, I had a good feeling each one of them could tell the good reverend every Turtle's name, color and weapon.

Right about that point, Bob's head turned towards the front of the house. I heard it, too. Sweetness was fussed about something out in the van.

"Excuse me," said Bob, getting up quickly. "I've got to check something."

Chrissie started to whimper. She'd heard Sweetness, too. I picked her up, smiled weakly at the group and followed Bob out.

Bob had a slight young man pinned against the side of the van.

"What are you doing in there?" Bob demanded.

"It sounded strange," said the young man. It was Will, still wearing his name tag. "I felt I'd better check it out. What have you got in there, anyway?"

"My cat." Bob let him go. "You want me to let her check you out?"

"That's no cat! It sounds like a lion."

"Lions roar. That is a Bengal tiger."

Will gaped. "You've got a little girl, and you keep a tiger?"

"Chrissie is a hell of a lot safer with Sweetness than your kids are with that shotgun on your fireplace."

"It's not loaded. I know how to keep guns."

"Then why are the shells right underneath it on the mantle?"

Will started back to the house. "It's my right to keep guns. And it's godless liberals that make it necessary. You might think about that."

"I hope you do when your kid gets blown away, playing games like Daddy." Bob grinned. "By the way, I don't think we'll be coming back."

We got in the van and took off.

"What was he doing?" I asked Bob as soon as Chrissie had fallen asleep between us.

"Going through the glove compartment." Bob leaves the van windows open when he's got Sweetness with him. This was the first time someone had stuck around. "Or starting to."

"You gotta give him credit for nerve."

"He hadn't looked in the back."

I groaned. "He thought it was some weird car alarm."

That got a chuckle out of Bob.

CHAPTER FOURTEEN

I put Chrissie to bed while Bob put Sweetness in her cage. We met back in the living room.

"You took your time," I told him from the couch.

"Did you and Sweetness make up?"

He chuckled. "Yes. We'll have to take Chrissie with us to the shoot tomorrow. I think it will be safer if she's in the van."

I sighed. "Bob, what's going to happen if they take Chrissie away from me?"

"That's why I've left it in God's hands. We have no control over what will happen with that. We have to believe that it will all work out."

I gazed at the blank television set and the tangle of cats sleeping on top. "I wish I could believe that."

"Do you?" It was a challenge, but not challenging. Bob sat down next to me. "Are you sure you really want to believe?"

"Why wouldn't I?"

"Because you have to trust, and when it doesn't work out, there you are, betrayed again."

I tried to laugh. "Nasty direct way you have of putting these things."

"Sometimes it's what needs to be said." Bob stretched and let his arm float down across my shoulders.

"Maybe," I said. "But it's easy for you.

Everything in your life has always worked out."

Bob snorted. "You don't see me wearing a Roman collar, do you?"

I looked at him. He was taking his turn staring at the blank TV. He seemed so…hurt. I'd never seen that before, or perhaps I'd been too wrapped up in my own problems to notice.

"Did you really want to be a priest?" I asked.

"I spent most of my life thinking I did." He noticed me, and squeezed me to his side. "Brenner, I don't want you thinking you messed up my vocation. You had nothing to do with it."

"Possibly in a metaphysical sense. But that all happened years ago, Bob. I'm not that fucked up."

He laughed. "You're not fucked up at all. Just hurt."

"Great. Damaged goods." I shifted in to get closer. "Is that why you like me so much?"

"No. I look past it. I…like you because you're funny. Because you're bright, and you're nurturing. Because you're a fighter, no matter how down you get, you're not out. And you're one of the bravest people I know. Even when you're most afraid, you hang tough and stand it down. I envy your guts, sometimes."

I sighed. "I don't feel that gutsy. I'm always faintly surprised when some kid or one of your cats backs down."

"I'll tell you a secret." Bob smiled. "I'm always a little surprised, too. You don't take cats for granted."

"Or humans."

Bob sighed. "Or humans, frequently. However, Brenner, I've got news for you. We don't all go around hurting others."

"So I trust, and when it doesn't work out, there I am, betrayed again."

"Or maybe it does work out, and then where are you?"

Standing around looking like a fool for

holding out so long."

"You don't give yourself much of a chance to be happy."

I blinked. "It's easier. That way you're not disappointed."

"We can't spend all our time happy."

"That's not what I'm saying. It's the something to look forward to. When you're in the valley, you know there's going to be times on the heights. I've spent so many years in the pits, I wouldn't know a height if I saw one."

"Better to bear those ills we have, than fly to others we know not of?"

"Something like that." I sighed. "Hamlet, Prince of Denmark."

Bob squeezed me again. "I loved sharing that movie with you, Brenner. And tearing it apart afterwards, analyzing, debating."

"That's why we saw it three times. Did we ever decide whether the incest was interpreted, or from the text?"

"I don't care. We'll argue about it some other time." He shifted so he could look me straight in the eye. "I'm much more interested in you right now."

His lips found mine, tender and exciting. I couldn't help thinking the seminary was not his thing.

"Brenner," he whispered. "The first time I kissed you was the first time I felt genuinely happy about not being a priest."

"Bob, why did you leave the seminary? I know you said it wasn't your vocation, but why not?"

He pressed his lips together, and pulled back a little.

"Boy, have I fallen into my own trap." He smiled guiltily. "I keep insisting on dragging out your deepest secrets. I shouldn't be surprised when you want to hear mine."

"Look, Bob, you don't have to."

"No." He kissed my forehead. "You have a right to know. I just don't tell people. I haven't even told my family."

"Then maybe you shouldn't."

He sighed. "I didn't leave the seminary, Brenner. I was asked to leave. Father Sebring called it a mutual decision. The only reason I agreed to it was that they weren't going to let me stay."

"What on earth happened? My god, Bob, it would have to have been something drastic. They're so short on priests and all."

"I did bring that point up. And Father said that was definitely regrettable." Bob got up and wandered. "You've noticed I have a temper. Well, when I was eighteen and nineteen, I wasn't very good at dealing with my anger, and I got into fist fights. Quite a few of them. One of the reasons I'm so good at street fighting."

"You've learned to deal with anger now. Why can't you go back?"

Bob shook his head. "It wasn't the fighting that was the problem. It was what caused it, what I was really angry at. Father Sebring tried to explain it to me. It took me eight years before it really sunk in. Like you, I'm a victim of my upbringing. I come from a very lovey-dovey, very affectionate family. I missed all the petting and cuddling. Priests don't get a lot of that, at least not enough for me to keep my equilibrium. I've had girlfriends pretty much constantly since I left. I lasted a whole two months between the time Jennifer broke up with me and I met you, and that's a long time for me."

I smiled. "And now look at you. You're a Eucharistic Minister. You're on the adult education board, the liturgy committee, you help with the altar boys, and anything else they need."

"I don't say mass." A bitter chuckle escaped him as he flopped back onto the couch. "That was what I was really after. The glory of being the big gun, saying mass. Not so much the mass, itself. The glory of being the one who did it. I had one hell of an over-blown ego in those days."

"Saint Bob?"

He winced. "Did Linda mention that by chance? I was a self-righteous prick. Kind of like Reverend Oakes. And I got taken down a few notches."

I slid over next to him. "Is that why it was so hard to face your family?"

"Yeah." He picked up my hand and kissed it. "They all expected it of me, and I had failed them. It took me years to shake the feeling that I was ultimately a failure. That's why I know Dr. Robbins so well."

"I thought that might be." I sat back, a little smug. "I'm glad. Not that you had to go to him. I always wondered, and I never wanted to ask. I didn't think you were hiding it. You just seemed so healthy, and I needed that."

"I am healthy. I wasn't then is all. And you're healthy, too, Brenner. You've only got a few emotional hurts that need healing. It's the difference between a broken bone and a disease like...arthritis."

I laughed. "I think I have more of congenital disorder, like a bone deformity."

"Right." Bob tackled me, then paused. He wanted to say something, but settled for kissing me instead.

The phone woke me up the next morning. After showering and getting dressed, I stumbled out to the kitchen. Dawn was just barely getting started. Bob chopped meat more vigorously than usual. I knew he was rushed because we had to get Sweetness to the video shoot, but this was more. He was angry.

I swallowed. "Did I get you to say too much last night?"

"What?" Bob all but dropped the cleaver.

"You seem so upset."

He relaxed a little. "No, Brenner. It has

nothing to do with you. Our friends from the cult have just started harrassing us by phone."

"I heard it ring."

"Well, the ringers are off, and the answering machine volume is at its lowest. I'll just check messages is all." He yawned. "It's not like we're going to be home anyway."

We got the animals fed in record time. Chrissie got herself up, bathed and dressed. If she was excited about going on a shoot with Sweetness, she didn't show it. She was supposed to start with Dr. Marshall the next day. I wondered how long it would take her to get over her wounds.

The video was being shot in a public park off of Wilshire. It wasn't all that far away, but there was plenty of traffic. We left at six fifteen and pulled in a little bit before eight.

Introductions were made all around, and then Bob and the director, Al Petrie, went into an extended discussion about what Sweetness would, or in most cases, would not do. It was about nine before Josh Ragner, heavy metal rock star, obliged us by hip hopping out of his trailer.

He was tall, not real skinny, except for his ass. That you could have slid into a junior's size one pair of jeans and zipped them shut without him lying down. Leather boots reached up past his knees, and he wore a patent leather vest over a bare chest. His hair had been freshly spiked to an all over halo which reached down his back further than my hair did. He wore leather bands and a variety of dark bracelets around his wrists, almost hiding the track marks. His hands were grimy, with black sludge under the nails. His eyes were red. He fidgeted and bounced about almost continuously. If he'd slept at all within the past twenty four hours, it hadn't been under his own influence.

I slipped up to Bob.

"Stoner. Big time," I said softly and nodded

at Ragner.

"Shit," Bob hissed back.

"Needle drugs, too. I'll buy lunch if he's not tripping on meth."

Ragner stretched his nostrils and sniffed.

"Make that coke."

Ragner spotted us, and scurried over. Bob and I were standing next to the van. The doors were open, but not the bars. Sweetness paced about, casually giving us a moment of her interest every so often, then moving on.

"So that's the tiger," said Ragner happily. "Fucking A. Here, kitty, kitty, kitty."

Sweetness favored him with a quick glare, then went on pacing.

"That kitty will take your face off if you're not careful," said Bob.

"Nah, animals fucking like me," boasted Ragner. "We'll get the playback fired up. It'll be so fucking happening."

"It won't." Bob's voice was firm. "It's in the contract. No sound, or no cat."

I moved around to where Sweetness could see me but Ragner couldn't.

"Look, you don't fucking understand," said Ragner. "This is my video. I call the shots. I don't have to have your fucking tiger."

"Fine. I get paid either way. But if you want a tiger in your video, you're stuck with mine, because there isn't another tiger in town that won't chew what little ass you have right off."

"I need my playback. How do you expect me to fucking play?"

Bob nodded at me. "You want to argue with her?"

I clicked the clicker to get Sweetness's attention, and gave her the signal to snarl. The nasty snarl.

Ragner backed off a little.

"Fuck."

Ooh, a variation on the theme.

"Well?" asked Bob.

I had Sweetness paw the air, with the really mean snarl. Petrie came up and announced that the sound people had rigged it so the playback could be done through ear plugs and headphones. Ragner fidgeted and okayed it.

The problem was that Ragner was so wired on whatever he was on. When he didn't calm down after an hour or so, I went back to my meth guess. I didn't see him doing any lines. Then again, he was probably doing both. I know. He should have been dead. Maybe that was the idea.

He got Sweetness riled at him once before lunch, by poking his hand through the bars on the van. She snapped at him. Probably the only time his drugs saved him. He was running so fast she missed. Bob threatened to take her home, but the assistant director promised to keep Ragner away.

Mid-afternoon in the summer is about the worst time in the world to be outside in Los Angeles. It was hot. The crew brought in sprayers, but the water evaporated almost before it could hit us. There were tents everywhere because palm trees don't make for much shade. Bob had the van parked under a tarp spread between two trees near the parking lot.

Chrissie went to sleep on the front seat.

At least we were done with all the takes we needed with Ragner. He still hung around, trying to tease Sweetness.

"I think next take I'll let her charge him," said Bob as we got ready for the final shot.

It was a running shot, and a complicated one because a dolly would have to follow Sweetness for several hundred feet while she ran after a truck carrying Bob, who would be calling her. They had laid the track out, and run the camera down it several times. We'd even run Sweetness down it once

144

for timing.

We ran her while the camera rolled. I rode with Bob, just in case. With Ragner being such an ass, and the way the crowds were collecting in spite of all the off-duty cops, Bob decided two of us had better be in reach at all times. Everything clicked along perfectly.

Except Petrie wasn't satisfied.

"We'll try it again," he announced.

Sighing, Bob and I walked Sweetness back to the starting spot. I put down a bowl of water for her. She lapped greedily. Then her head popped up. She listened, then growled, and started for the van. Bob tried to jerk her back.

The high pitched scream of electric guitar at its distorted worst crashed through the park. Ragner's band pounded and screeched from the massive speakers that had been set up for the playback Bob would not allow. Ragner danced nearby, his arms in the air, just begging Sweetness to make cat food out of him.

Which is precisely what Sweetness tried to do. Her sweet, mellow temperament had taken a beating that day, and she was going to give some back. Yowling, her head twisted and snapped as she lunged. I landed on my seat. Bob lost his grip on her collar, but stayed standing. He grabbed her again, and yelled her back.

As if all that weren't bad enough, the crowd that we'd tried so hard to keep away moved in closer, then panicked. Women screamed. People ran all over. I scrambled up and got on Sweetness's other side. Between the two of us, we pushed her to the van. When we got there, she yowled as if wounded and jumped right in.

Bob didn't notice. He locked the bars and the back doors very quickly, then went after Petrie and Ragner.

"Ragner, you fucking idiot!" Bob bellowed. He

was really, really angry. "If you want to fucking kill yourself, then fucking do it. I say good riddance. But not with one of my cats, and not where you're going to take others with you. Petrie, I'm filing damages, and you're paying for the insurance, because I'll be damned before I do. I told you to keep that asshole under control."

My arm started hurting. Looking down, I saw blood ooze from a long scratch. I went to the front of the van.

"Bob!" I screamed.

That stopped him. He came running up. Tires screeched from the parking lot. The crowd had settled down and was enjoying the fireworks, and blocking my view.

"What's the matter?" Bob yelped.

I jumped onto the bumper. "Chrissie's gone!"

Over the heads, I saw a light colored car pull into traffic.

"It's the Mercedes." Tears poured down my cheeks as I jumped down. "The one that got Halford. They've got Chrissie. I know they do."

"That can't be." Bob scrambled onto the bumper, but couldn't see anything. "Are you sure it's the same car?"

"How many other light colored Mercedes have we seen leaving the scene when somebody turns up missing?"

Bob got a grip on himself by gripping me. He almost knocked the wind out of me. The location cops ambled up.

It took forever to get everything straightened out.

Petrie was beside himself. His schedule had just been shot to hell, and he didn't dare ask Bob for an extra take. Ragner's manager, on the other hand, was thrilled to death. Ragner's death wish and a rampaging tiger? You could almost hear the cash register bells ringing in the manager's brain. Better

146

yet, a radio station's car had just arrived when it all happened.

The only nice thing about it was that Ragner and his manager kept the radio people tied up, so they didn't get wind of the kidnapping. The location cops called in a patrol unit that didn't show up for a half hour. They weren't too impressed with who we believed to be the culprits. After all, I didn't get the license number, and who knew what kind of car it was I'd seen. They told us they'd turn it in to the detectives, and asked if I wanted an ambulance for my arm which continued to ooze blood. We declined.

After the cops left, Bob worked out money with Petrie and the producer. They gave me a hefty check, and I signed a release, then we got in the van and left. I opened my mouth to speak. Bob held up his hand.

"Let's get your arm taken care of first," he said. "We've both got theories. I just want to think over mine first."

I nodded.

CHAPTER FIFTEEN

One hundred and twelve stitches it took to patch me together. The cut wasn't that long, but Dr. Kimble decided she wanted to do some embroidery. Her way of avoiding a scar, she said.

Bob, at least, remained pretty even-tempered.

Thank God, because I was five seconds short of a basket case. The pain pills left me a little woozy, and I napped all the way back to Tujunga. Bob stopped at a Taco Bell for dinner. We ate at the house.

I remember Bob's messages went on for a long time. All of them were from the cult. At least they hadn't followed us that day. We'd ditched them pretty quickly in the morning.

"What are the odds of New Jerusalem having a light colored Mercedes?" I asked as we munched on our burritos.

"With a license plate number almost like the Reverend's?" Bob shook his head and tabasco on his meal. "It's possible, I suppose. Stranger things have happened. But remember, the cult did not seem to know where Patricia Halford was, or that she was dead. I don't think they kidnapped her, nor do I think they kidnapped Chrissie today. I didn't see hide nor polyester of a cheap suit, and I was looking for them."

"Neither did I. But why would Reverend Oakes kidnap Chrissie? Or Patricia Halford, for that matter?"

"Why would Will try to search my van? There's something funny going on with that group, and it isn't just standard fundamentalist narrow mindedness."

Something slowly turned in my brain. "Bob, do you remember when we talked with Dr. Chritener, and he seemed so worried about amateurs who try to debrief cult members?"

"Yeah. So?"

"What if that's what's happening? The Reverend is into debriefing cult members. He kidnaps them, then tries to save them."

"Then what happened to Patricia Halford?"

I shrugged. "I don't know. Maybe she escaped and was picked up by some weirdos. But dollars will get you doughnuts, we'll find Chrissie with Reverend Oakes."

Bob thought this one over. "We'll need to get inside their house, possibly their yard."

"And how are you going to do it?"

Bob got up and grabbed the phone. "The magic of the movies."

He dialed and got his sister. The pills were making me tired again, so I snoozed through the conversation. I'm still not sure how Bob bribed her, but Sue agreed to set it up and meet us there the next day.

Somehow, I stumbled to the living room. Pain, fuzziness, thoughts drifted along. In the peace of the evening, and with analysis for the moment either taken care of or impossible, the enormity of the day slowly sank in. I had fucked up royally.

Bob found me crying on the couch.

"It's my fault," I sobbed. "I should've kept a closer eye on her. I shouldn't have left her in the van."

"Brenner, it's not your fault." He sat down on the end of the couch and pulled me into his lap. "Chrissie was asleep. We had no reason to believe there was any danger from the cult, let alone these new guys."

"I still should've watched her."

"You were watching her. Who knew Ragner was going to push things as far as he did? And if you hadn't been there, he'd probably be dead, and we'd have to destroy Sweetness."

"Great. He's alive, and heaven only knows what's happening to Chrissie. Hasn't that poor child suffered enough?"

"We'll find her, Brenner."

His kisses were soft and reassuring. And more. As his lips tickled me behind my ear, I nudged his hand onto my breasts. He gently squeezed and sighed in pure contentment.

"Brenner, this is not a habit we can afford to get into," he muttered with no intention of stopping.

"You don't want me," I complained petulantly.

He wriggled around to face me. "Yes, I do want you. But I don't think you're ready to deal with all the complications and the commitment making love implies."

"So blame it all on me, why don't you?"

"I'm not blaming it on you. I don't know how you've dealt with sex in the past—"

"I haven't." I snorted. Those damn pills had really done something to me. Words poured out of my mouth and I couldn't stop them. "I haven't done a damn thing. Would you believe I'm twenty-seven years old, and I'm still a virgin. Shit, even the 'I'll take anything' types left me alone."

"Are you sure you've let anyone close enough?"

"So that's my fault, too!" I stumbled to my feet. "I thought you religion types were supposed to like virtue and virginity."

I couldn't tell if Bob was genuinely confused or trying to plan his next move. Heaven knows, I'd gone past rational. He got up and put his hands on my shoulders.

"Brenner, you are an attractive woman. And

150

I like the fact that you're a virgin."

"Typical macho attitude." I pulled away, or tried rather.

Bob hung on. "No. I shouldn't be embarrassed, but I'm a virgin, too. I don't advertise it, even though there is no reason to be ashamed of it."

I thought that one over. "Are you scared to make love to me?"

"A little," he admitted softly. "That's not the whole reason. Morals are mostly why."

"And the fact that I'm an ugly, bad-assed, bull dyke bitch."

He shook me, really angry. "Don't you ever, ever say that about yourself again. Don't even dare think it! I swear, I ought to take you over my knee. And if I ever hear you say it again, I will."

I wrenched away. "You'll have to fight me." I laughed. "Real feminine, huh?"

"What is it going to take? How I can I prove it to you?"

"Make love to me."

He hesitated. "I just might. If I thought it might do any real good, I'd do it."

"Yeah, right."

"You don't really believe I want to." He was pissed.

I glared at him. "What am I supposed to think? You keep hiding behind your goddamned morals, and saying you want me, and you won't do shit about it."

"I'm ready to beat it out of you. Do you really want it that way? I want you, Brenner. I went past desire a year and a half ago. There are times when that's all I can think about. I want to pin you to that couch, and plunge myself into you, and thrash it out until we're both sweaty and screaming and exploding."

I caught my breath. "Then what in heaven's name is stopping you?"

"You." He caught my hands, and our fingers interlocked.

"How many times have I asked you—"

"And never once offered me your love." His grip tightened as I sniffed. "I know it's there, Brenner."

"It's not."

"It's all locked up. We'll get it."

"It's not going to happen, Bob."

"Yes, it will, because I'm not giving up. You mean too much to me."

"I don't want to mean that much to you! Why do you do this to me? It's not fair."

"I love you, Brenner."

"Bob, no."

"You're not stopping me. I'm going to say what I feel, and you're going to have to hear it." He came toward me.

I backed up. "Bob, don't."

He pressed forward. "I can't take it anymore. I love you passionately, lyrically, completely."

"But I can't." I backed into the wall.

"I don't care." He leaned against the wall, his arms on either side of me. "I've had enough walking on eggshells around your problems. It doesn't matter to me that you can't find the words yet, or that you're too afraid to make a commitment. I still love you, and I'm going to say so, and keep on saying so, even after you get it through your thick skull that my feelings are for real and that you are desirable." He pulled my braid from behind my back and undid the band holding it together. "Because you are. You're beautiful, and not just to me." His hands spread my hair about my shoulders. "I can't contain it anymore. I love you, Brenner."

He kissed, or rather, we kissed, hard and full. His hips pressed into mine, and I felt a long, hard ridge that wasn't his button fly. It was with no small reluctance that we pulled away to go to our individual beds.

I had to respect that he would not violate his beliefs for me. But, damn, I was horny. My lower gut filled with a dull ache, one that would only be relieved by getting it off. So, I did. I hadn't done it in years. In high school, I'd been obsessive about it. In college I decided it wasn't all that healthy and broke the habit. I wondered if Bob was doing it, and trying to picture him at it brought the release.

Sleep came pretty quickly. But like any sleep that's been helped along by drugs or booze, it didn't last.

The dream was bizarre in that it was so utterly realistic.

There was a brush fire in the canyon. Bob had started evacuation procedures. He always starts packing up long before the ranch becomes actually endangered. With as many animals as he has, he has to if he's going to get them out in time.

The neighbors had the cattle truck they share already at the barn, and they were loading up the hoof stock. Bob had me putting the caged birds in the van, with his original artwork. The big cats were already caged on the flatbed trailer, which had been hooked up to the pick-up. I got the dogs in their cages on the trailer while Bob rounded up as many of the small cats as he could. Then he got a smaller cage, and trilling and chirping, called the small birds in the aviary into the cage.

I could smell the smoke as we pulled away. At the bottom of the hill, Bob left the pick up. He had forgotten something. I ran after him. The ranch was in flames. Bob plunged right in. I bolted upright.

I was awake and sitting up in bed. There was a dim smell of smoke, but nothing I could put my finger on. I looked out front. Nothing. The dogs were barking, and the cats kicked up a fuss, but then they settled down rather quickly. I heard faint mooing, which meant the sheep and cattle had come in from the hills, which they didn't usually do.

Nervous and uneasy, I got out of bed. The rest of the house was dark. I looked out the sliding glass doors in the living room. Outside was black as charcoal. Somewhere above, the sheriff's department helicopter beat its way through the sky. I saw the spotlight's beam reach down into the hills, but couldn't see what it was aimed at.

A voice on a radio said something and cut out. I followed it. Static rustled.

"Base one, fire is out. Unit twelve will remain to check embers," a voice crackled softly from behind the door to Bob's bedroom. "Unit three, over."

I heard Bob sigh and roll over. Softly, I opened the door. A tiny red light glowed on the night stand. A police scanner. It made sense, with the fire danger pretty high in the canyon. Bob slept on his side in the middle of the bed, completely covered by a sheet.

I looked out his window. But for the night, I could have seen whatever the chopper was looking at in the hills. A white light bobbed up and out. It looked far enough away to not be on Bob's property.

I started for the door and the guest room. The black hole that was the hall terrified me. I couldn't go out there. I shut the door quickly, but silently. I looked back at Bob.

"Bob?" I asked softly.

He grunted.

"Bob, this might sound silly, but I can't sleep. I had this awful dream."

"Mm-hm."

"I'm scared to be alone. Can I sleep here?"

"Sure." Or what sounded like it.

I picked up the extra pillow off the floor, and crawled into bed on the side nearest the window. I lay on my side facing away from him. He slipped up behind me. His arm wound over me, and he squeezed and fondled my breasts. So much for release. I could feel his penis long and hard nestled in the crack of my buttocks. He sighed again, snorted and fell still, his breathing deep and even. Sound asleep.

Just my luck. He still stayed hard, though. I have reason to believe it was just male anatomy. My brothers often wandered about the house half asleep and fully erect trying to find the bathroom in the middle of the night while I stayed up and read.

Bob was gone when I woke up the next morning. I cleaned up as much as I could in the other bathroom, (I couldn't shower because of my stitches) and got dressed. When I got to the kitchen, he was there, chopping cat food. He was embarrassed. All right, so was I. I don't wear much to bed, just a t-shirt and undies. He sacked out in his boxers.

"I'm sorry about last night," I said quickly. "I got scared. I had a bad dream."

Bob flushed. "I thought I was having a very good one. I really did think I was dreaming. The old pacemaker got a workout when I woke up and saw you there."

"I'm really sorry about that. I shouldn't have."

Bob put down the cleaver and washed his hands.

"I don't care, Brenner." He put his arms around me. "It was kind of nice, actually."

"Are we being silly, or what? Last night we're talking about making love, and this morning we're all embarrassed because we caught each other in our underwear."

Laughing, Bob took my face in his hands and kissed me soundly. It was a delightful moment completely shattered when the front gate buzzed.

Groaning, Bob went to the den and looked out front.

"It's somebody from the Sheriff's department," he said coming out.

I followed him outside.

"Are you..." The deputy checked his notes. "Robert Zebrinski?"

"Yeah." Bob opened the gate.

The deputy walked in. His name badge said R. Vasquez. He was of average size and rather good looking.

"There was a little trouble out here last night, on the western edge of your property," said Vasquez.

"There was?" asked Bob. "I didn't see anything."

"Was it a fire?" I asked. "I heard the helicopter, but I couldn't see what it was looking for."

Vasquez looked at me. "You are?"

"A friend," I said quickly. "Brenda Finnegan. I was having some trouble at my apartment. Bob's been letting me stay here."

"Heard he's been having trouble, too," said Vasquez.

Bob cut in. "Was it a fire? I had a really weird dream about one."

Vasquez nodded. "You lucked out. The chopper was patrolling when they lit it. Got the units out right away, so it only burned half an acre. Wind was blowing away from this place anyway."

"Lit it?" I asked. "You mean it was arson?"

"Yep. Conservation corps spotted the bottle this morning. Somebody had tossed it over the fence."

I looked at Bob. As if we didn't know who.

"I came up to see if you could let the fire marshall in to get it, and to find out if you saw anything."

"Not anything that would help," I said. "But we're being harassed by a religious cult. They've been violent before."

Vasquez nodded. "New Jerusalem. We got the car. But the guys in it couldn't have done it. LAPD had them at County for harrassing tenants at an apartment building in West Hollywood at the time of the fire. They weren't bailed out until two hours later."

"But the car?" asked Bob.

"It had the incendiary materials in it. Just not the guys who set the fire." Vasquez shrugged. "About the fire marshall."

Bob checked his watch. "We've got to take off at eleven. If he can get here before nine thirty, I can take him up there."

A white official car pulled up.

"Looks like him now," said Vasquez. He waved the car forward.

"I'll feed the cats," I told Bob softly, and went in to do it.

<h1 style="text-align:center">CHAPTER SIXTEEN</h1>

To say the cats were touchy that morning would be an understatement. Especially Sweetness. She was fussed and worried and more restless than her metaphorical cousin. Mango, her next door cage mate, was even more surly than usual, and swatted at Sweetness every time she went past. When Bob announced that it was time to go meet Sue, Sweetness let out the most pitiful yowl.

He stopped and turned to her. "I'm sorry, Sweetness, but we've got to get going."

Sweetness yowled again and butted at the cage door. Bob stepped back in surprise.

"She can't understand what we're saying," I said.

"No." Bob put his hand in the cage. Sweetness lowered her head, and Bob scratched between her ears. "She misses Chrissie, though, and she doesn't want to be left alone." He shrugged. "We'll just have to take her with us."

"Oh, great. The Oakes know your van."

"They know us." He got out the leash and collar.

Sweetness rode at the front of the van, literally breathing down Bob's neck through the screen. We met Sue at a service station near the Oakes home.

She grinned when she saw me. "Brenner, you let your hair loose. It looks great."

158

I flushed and glared sideways at Bob. He'd washed it for me in his kitchen sink, after we'd fed the animals, and then had refused to braid it. He claimed I looked better with it down.

"You guys lucked out," she announced. "Mrs. Oakes is going to be out all day. She's going to have the maid let us in."

"That's too perfect," I said.

Bob just grinned. He says he doesn't believe in miracles, he relies on them. I have no idea what patron saint he'd tapped for this one, but I was grateful.

Sue rode with us in the van. The street was deserted when we pulled up. Lucky for us. As we got out of the van, Sweetness kicked up a ruckus. I thought Bob was going to shush her, but he turned thoughtful.

"I'm bringing her in," he said finally.

"Bob—" began Sue.

"How?" I asked at the same time.

Bob held up his hand. "Brenner, you'll be the director. You want to see how the tiger looks in this setting. Sue, what did you tell them this shoot was for?"

"An in-house commercial for a bank," she said. "That way if they never see anything like what we say we're doing, it won't matter. They wouldn't see it anyway."

The Oakes' maid was a Hispanic woman with "no inglés." It figured. I'd have put money on her being illegal. My half-assed Spanish convinced her that we were the movie people. She balked when she saw Sweetness, but didn't protest. Odd how Sweetness has that effect on people. After showing us her kitchen, she went back to her rooms and turned the TV up loud to some Spanish soap opera.

The house was perfectly clean and utterly benign. Nor was there any trace of Chrissie, or anything that might indicate a debriefing had taken place there.

We finished up in the study. Sweetness snorted disconsolately.

"Now what?" asked Bob.

I pulled a pair of rubber gloves from my pocket. Bob keeps them for minor medical emergencies with his cats.

"It's time to start opening drawers," I said, pulling the gloves on. Bob reached for the desk. "Not with bare hands! Shit, Bob, even my dumbest students know better than that."

"I don't know," said Sue. "Isn't searching drawers illegal?"

"It depends on how you interpret privacy laws." I looked through a side drawer, fairly certain that what I was doing was illegal.

Bob went to the window and watched out front.

Sweetness plopped down at his feet and knocked over a potted palm.

"We have to find Chrissie," he said, righting the pot. "We have every reason to believe these people have her, and the police have already blown us off about them."

"Damn," I muttered. "Nothing. Wait. The top center drawer won't open."

I grabbed a letter opener off the top of the desk.

Sue's jaw dropped. "Are you going to force it?"

"It's a snap," I said poking into the hole. "One of my students showed me when some of the others had locked my keys in my desk as a joke. He won't even know I've done it."

Sure enough, the lock gave. I found what I wanted almost immediately. It was a thin black journal book.

"The Record of Our Mission to Save Those Imprisoned by the Cults," was written on the inside cover page.

"Holy shit, he is debriefing," I said.

"Then where..?" Bob turned into the room. "We haven't checked the back yard yet, have we?"

"Let's go," said Sue.

They left while I slipped the journal into my t-shirt and re-locked the desk. I replaced the letter opener, and hurried out after them.

The yard was filled with lush greenery. A steep hillside rose up from a narrow expanse of patio, covered in ivy, with boughs of trees and other shrubbery leaving leafy messes all over the place. The place was surrounded by a wooden fence that got shorter as it went up the hill.

With a sudden snarl, that's right where Sweetness headed. She tore the leash out of Bob's hands. Bob and I were on her in a second. Not that it did any good. Sweetness was really determined, and had three hundred and sixty pounds on her side.

She scrambled over the fence, dragging Bob and me with her, into Will Whatshisname's backyard. It was considerably larger, and had medium sized cabana next to a sparkling swimming pool. Sweetness went straight for the cabana.

She prowled around it, growling and complaining. Bob looked at me, then peered in a set of sliding glass doors.

"Shit," he muttered. "It looks like they've got an electric chair in there."

Something white on the ground next to the cabana's wall caught my eye. I picked it up.

"Bob," I hissed, trying not to cry.

He came over and took it. He looked at the dot letters and nearly choked up.

"Her barrette," he whispered.

"She was so happy about having her name on it, too," I said.

"Well, she's not here now." Bob grabbed Sweetness's leash. "Something tells me Sweetness would be breaking down their door if she was."

I nodded. Sweetness seemed satisfied, and went with us docilely, as if her behavior had been perfectly circumspect all along. Damned cat.

Back at the Oakes', we stopped by the maid's room to let her know we were leaving. The door was open.

We waved at her, and she ignored us. I didn't think she'd say anything about the tiger. She probably spoke English a hell of a lot better than she let on. Her revenge against the white bitch who had hired her. I didn't blame her one damned bit.

Bob, at least, had the sense not to ask me about the journal until after Sue had taken off.

"Did you see anything about Chrissie, or Patricia Halford?" he asked as we headed back to Tujunga.

"Not yet."

"Yet?" Bob spared me a nervous glance.

"Yeah, yet. I took the damned thing."

"Brenner, that's theft!"

"And he's guilty of kidnapping. I didn't have time to look at it there. I'm hoping it'll tell us where to find Chrissie."

"And what happens when he discovers it's missing?"

"There's not one iota of proof that we have it. He'll need to give a lot more evidence before the police can get a search warrant on us. There's no real evidence we were even there."

"What about the maid?"

"She's not going to say anything, even if she could. And five will get you ten, Oakes doesn't speak Spanish, at least not well enough for her to implicate us, and we didn't give her our names, anyway."

"We did have Sweetness with us. Not too many people wander around with tigers in tow."

I shrugged. "That's assuming Oakes knows enough Spanish for him to understand when she tells him. He's paranoid enough, he might think she did

162

it, but I doubt it. After all, how would she know that it was valuable if she couldn't read it? And I doubt Oakes would think she can read."

Bob remained skeptical. However, we largely forgot about the journal when we got back to the ranch.

A large eighteen wheeler rig was about to back into the gate as we pulled up.

Bob opened the gate, and pulled around into the drive, then stopped the van and jumped out. I scrambled out myself.

"You Robert Zebrinski?" demanded a tall, whiney man in a Fish and Game uniform.

"Yes," answered Bob. "What the hell is going on?"

"Officer Wilkie, Fish and Game Department. We're here to impound some large cats you have on your property."

"Whoa!" Bob's face went white, then red. "You wait just one damned minute. I'm permitted to keep those cats."

"The permits have been temporarily revoked." Wilkie sniffed. "We've received several complaints that you've been mistreating the animals."

"This is a setup," snapped Bob. "I have been working cats for nine years, and there has never been a complaint filed, let alone proven, against me."

Wilkie shrugged. "Here's the order."

Bob took the paper and read it. "Superior court. Damn."

I grabbed it. "Bob, this is a court in Fresno."

"So?"

"Who else is in Fresno?"

It clicked. "The Temple of the New Jerusalem."

Bob turned on Wilkie. "What office do you work out of?"

"Fresno. So?"

"Don't you think it's a little odd that we're down here in Los Angeles?"

Wilkie shrugged. "I've got my orders. Now, will you clear the van?"

"Hold on." Bob swallowed. "This order doesn't say it has to happen today. I work with the LA office all the time. You know Deanna Swanson?"

"I've heard of her."

"I'm going to go call her now. She'll come out and prove to you that this is a mistake. That I'm being set up. Okay?"

Wilkie frowned. "You've got one hour, then I'm calling the sheriff in and having you busted for contempt of court."

Bob all but ran for the house. Deanna was in her office for a change. He read her names and numbers, then hung up and dialed again. Dr. Mel Stevenson agreed to come out immediately. Bob hung up.

"They can't do this to me," he groaned, his eyes filling. "They can't, damn it. Not my cats."

My heart pounded, but I hugged him anyway.

"They won't," I whispered. "We'll fight them tooth and nail. We'll get the cats back if they have to take them. You've got tons of friends, Bob. Even the worst asshole in the industry won't say you treat your cats badly."

"What about Ragner yesterday?"

"There's a whole video crew that can testify Ragner was begging for it. And they will. I've never heard anybody say anything bad about you. The only things they've ever cussed you out for is taking care of your cats before whatever stupid project they were working on."

Bob squeezed me so tightly my ribs hurt.

Mel Stevenson arrived in record time. After proving to Wilkie that he was indeed the noted zoologist and veterinary scientist, he set to convincing Wilkie that whatever complaints had been made against Bob were completely groundless. Wilkie just got more sensory judgemental and stuck to his orders like epoxy.

Deanna Swanson arrived just as Wilkie started to call the Sheriff's Department. Her arrival only set him more firmly in his resolve, although he aborted his call.

"Where's the order?" Deanna demanded. She's a small woman, with fluffy brown hair. Don't let that fool you. She regularly backs down wild cougars. She could make mincemeat of a whiney colleague without breathing hard.

Bob handed it to her. She read it and groaned.

"Wilkie, you idiot! This is an inspect and impound. You're supposed to verify the complaint first."

"It was verified," said Wilkie with a haughty sniff.

"By who?" snapped Deanna. "Where's your paperwork?"

"The complainant was very specific. And he swore under oath that he'd witnessed the abuses."

Deanna all but exploded. "You bleeding fool! Haven't you ever heard of perjury? Now get this semi rig out of here before I skin you alive."

"But what about the order?" whined Wilkie.

"Where's your paperwork?" Deanna didn't wait for his answer, but leapt into the semi's cab, and got it herself. She scribbled, clipped the court order to the clipboard it was all on, then jumped out and shoved it all at Mel Stevenson. "Mel, will you verify this?"

"Gladly." Mel scribbled.

Deanna took it back when he was done, and shoved it all at Wilkie.

"There's your blessed order," she told him. "And if you ever come down to my district again, I will have you out of uniform so fast your hairpiece will fall off."

Wilkie's hand flew to his head. Flushing, he glanced at Bob and me and Mel, then ran for the eighteen wheeler.

Bob didn't start breathing again until the rumble of the truck had died off into the distance.

"Thanks, Deanna," he sighed. "Why don't you guys come in. I'll get us some coffee."

"I'll make it," I said quickly. "You sit down and get your wind back."

He was bushwhacked. Nary a snicker or glint of hope lit up his eyes. And, damn him, I was so worried I was sorry there wasn't.

Deanna and Mel seemed rather weary, themselves. They flopped into the kitchen chairs almost as listlessly as Bob did when he came in after putting Sweetness in her cage. I silently went about getting the coffee maker going.

"It's a damned good thing you thought to call Mel," said Deanna. "I couldn't have signed off those papers without him."

"I don't get it." Mel shook his head. "What do these people hope to accomplish by this kind of harassment?"

"Remember Chrissie?" said Bob. "They want her back. We can't because they are abusive as hell."

"All right, I won't suggest that," said Deanna. "But, Bob, you've got to do something. The calls have been coming in fast and furious. Sacramento is beginning to ask questions. I can't come running out here all the time just because some religious crazies have a grudge against you. If this keeps up, Sacramento will pull your permits."

"Deanna, you know they're lying through their teeth," pleaded Bob.

"I know that. Mel knows that. Sacramento doesn't, and when they see this many complaints, they begin to wonder. You can hardly blame them."

Mel shook his head. "The complaints are ridiculous and groundless, Deanna. Personally, I think we should have conducted Wilkie on a tour of the grounds so he could see that Bob treats his cats

166

well."

"It wouldn't have done any good, Mel. That asshole would've followed through on orders against James Herriot. A single turd in a cage would convince him."

"So what do I do now?" groaned Bob. "I can't let them take the cats. I've got to make a living, let alone the emotional investment."

Deanna reached over and patted his hand. "Don't give up hope, Bob. They're not impounded yet."

"I'll have to talk to Sacramento, myself," said Mel. "Doug Michaelson is a friend of mine. He should be able to keep this under control. Bob, you got a phone?"

It's amazing what high connections a lowly zoology Prof. has. Mel got through to the head of Fish and Game with almost no waiting. They chatted golf scores for a minute or two, then Mel got down to brass tacks and let Michaelson know what was going on. Mel insisted on an all-department memo that would keep any complaints against Bob from being filed.

"Michaelson says it will be out first thing in the morning," said Mel as he hung up.

"Then it will be on my desk before noon," said Deanna, in awe. "Shit. I couldn't have done that."

"Bob, our asses are really on the line with this one," said Mel. "I only pushed for it because I know I can trust you not to abuse it."

"It's one hell of a time to do it," sighed Bob. "I don't know if you heard, but Sweetness charged Josh Ragner yesterday."

"Isn't he some heavy metal rock star?" asked Mel.

"And not that good to boot," said Deanna.

Mel nodded. "I heard about it on the radio. The witnesses said Ragner had been teasing the tiger all day, and that the trainers had it under complete control long before it could have hurt anybody. No problem. You're just damned lucky, Bob."

Bob glanced skyward. "Yeah."

We chit-chatted from there for a while. Deanna took off pretty quickly. Mel and Bob went out to look at the cats. I stayed inside and started dinner. Mel ate with us, lingering on a while longer after we finished. I didn't say anything, but I wanted him gone.

I had a journal to get through. Bob finally saw him off, then helped me finish the dishes.

"I'm sorry," Bob said as we drifted into the living room. "But I figured I'd better let him stick around if he wanted. He's all that's standing between us and getting the cats taken away."

"For the moment, at any rate," I replied. I gave in and held him.

"I can't let them do it." Bob shook. "Of all the things to attack, they had to go after my cats."

"Your cats are safe." I pulled away, and went over to the lamp table.

I pulled open the drawer and got out his prayer book and rosary.

"Why don't you go take a walk?" I pressed them into his hands.

"Brenner..." Momentarily lost for words, Bob pulled me into his arms and pressed his mouth against mine. "I love you so much."

He squeezed me once more, then stalked off through the sliding glass doors. I took several deep breaths, hoping to calm my own fears. I settled for reading the journal.

CHAPTER SEVENTEEN

I do not read horror novels. I spook far too easily.

Reverend Oakes' journal had my flesh crawling within seconds. It had begun with a dream. Oakes believed it was God telling him to rescue poor souls held captive by demon cults. Then Mr. and Mrs. Halford joined his flock and that proved it.

Will Ackert also heard the call, and became very excited about the project. He was the one who suggested that they keep the project quiet so as not to alert the forces of evil.

How they found Patricia Halford so quickly amounted to pure dumb luck. Like me, they had gone through the phone book, asking around. Apparently, someone at New Jerusalem slipped up, and let out that one of their members had once been Patricia Halford. Will and Oakes took it as God blessing their mission. From there it was just a matter of following Halford around until they got a chance at her. Oakes drove. Will had enlisted the help of another of Oakes' flock, a Ben Spence.

Oakes insisted that Patricia's parents not know of the recovery, although he had taken the precaution of notifying the police that she had been found. Oakes cursed himself for his lack of faith, but still could not bring himself to raise the Halfords' hopes until the mission was a complete success, and they could restore Patricia to them, newly healed.

They kept Patricia in the Ackert cabana, tied down to prevent escape. Although he wrote as though his inspiration came straight from God, Oakes had obviously been exposed to behavior modification methods somewhere. The plan was to withhold all but the very least needed for Halford to survive until she acknowledged Jesus as her true savior. Then she would be given food and drink as a reward. Any time she spouted out with cult propaganda, she would be beaten.

"For Scripture is quite clear," wrote Oakes. "'Withhold not correction from the child: for if thou beatest him with the rod, he shall not die. Thou shalt beat him with the rod, and shalt deliver his soul from hell.' and again in Isaiah 'For the fitches are not threshed with a threshing instrument, neither is a cart wheel turned upon the cummin; but the fitches are beaten out with a staff, and the cummin with a rod.'"

For some reason, Oakes and Will settled for their hands. They didn't really make any progress.

"Patricia seems mostly unaffected by the blows," read the journal. "She doesn't cry out at all, nor even flinches."

Surprise, surprise. I guess they didn't know that much about how New Jerusalem worked. On the second day after the kidnapping, Wednesday, things got gruesome.

"I'm afraid Will got a little too rough," Oakes wrote. "He's so zealous for Patricia's salvation. He accidently broke her nose. From there on, I insisted on handling Patricia, myself. She remained stubborn. I had to resort to several very strong slaps across her face. Her head whipped about so. I don't know how it could have happened. God forgive me, I wanted her to see His Light so badly. She went limp. Blood foamed in her mouth. It was Will who realized she was dead. I didn't kill her. I couldn't have. The Lord must have realized that she was weak and took her

170

to Him, lest life here on earth again tempt her."

"I'm frightened," read the next entry. "Will insisted on taking care of the body. He said it would not be fair to the Halfords if Patricia were never found, so he arranged that she would be. I dreamt of blood on my hands, but that can only be Satan trying to weaken me in my resolve. The Lord has allowed this to happen for a purpose."

The bastard officiated at Patricia's funeral, and received peace in doing so. There were no more entries until the Wednesday Bob and I showed up at the bible study, a week after Patricia's death.

"Another victim desperately needing help has been dropped into our midst. The young couple with whom Patricia was talking the night we rescued her came to our bible study. Will seems certain they are members of the Temple of New Jerusalem. Why else would there be a tiger in their van? Yes, a real, living tiger. It must be part of some profane ritual. They claim that the young man is an animal trainer. Perhaps he is, but there is no doubt that they have come searching for Patricia, perhaps to take her back to their wickedness. I thank God, Almighty, that she is safe from their clutches. They had a child with them, which they called Chrissie. She is dressed as other children are, but I am convinced by her behavior that she has been brainwashed by the cult. Will says that he will go to the Film Office tomorrow to see if what the couple said is true about them filming tomorrow. With God's grace, we shall make another rescue."

Oakes was thrilled to death with his second success in the kidnapping biz. Debriefing Chrissie proved even easier. She agreed to everything. Another big surprise. That's right. They didn't know how New Jerusalem worked.

"We have called the Halfords. They have responded in the most charitable way, and agreed to take the little girl into their home. I will deliver her tomorrow morning. I should go to bed, but the pure joy of our success keeps me awake. God has truly blessed this mission, even with the tragedy. I know now that Patricia Halford sleeps in Christ, only for a little while, until the last great trumpet calls us to our Heavenly Father, and Christ returns in triumph."

I certainly hoped so. I wanted to send Oakes the other way.

The journal answered all the questions that were left. The problem was what to do about the answers.

Chrissie was safe. Possibly. Mr. Halford was supposed to believe in not sparing the rod either. At least we knew where she was. Well, we had every reason to believe she was there. Of course, that also meant Oakes was going to discover the journal was missing pretty damned soon.

Ah, the journal. The fact was I had stolen it, so turning it in to the police would make things rather sticky. The LA Unified School District doesn't seem to mind if their students have police records, but they object when their teachers do. It wouldn't have done any good anyway, because it was illegal evidence, which would never be allowed in court. But something had to be done.

I was still trying to puzzle out what when Bob came in. I told him the whole, ugly story.

"So Oakes killed Patricia Halford?" he asked, slightly amazed.

"Looks like. There's no reason he'd lie to his journal, and he seems to have rationalized his way around it. The question is what do we do?"

Bob sat back and thought about it. "You know, we may just be able to set up Oakes and get the cult off our necks."

Trust Bob to come up with something perfectly legal, and yet wonderfully tricky. We decided to worry about getting Chrissie back until after we had Oakes in the bag. If we failed, it could have made things awkward, not to mention impossible, as far as getting her back. Or worse, we could have led New Jerusalem right to her.

Sergeant Griswell was reluctant to cooperate.

"But, see, we have no evidence," I told him the next morning on the phone. "All I have is a barrette that we accidently found in a yard we weren't supposed to be in. We're still guessing about Halford getting killed there, but it makes sense."

He finally agreed. Getting the gang from New Jerusalem in position was easy. We just let them follow us as we left the ranch that afternoon.

We took the Miata down to Santa Monica, and found a parking spot not ten feet from where the meeting was set up, with time still on the meter.

Oakes would have said God was smiling on us. Bob just thanked Saint Anthony.

There is a park that runs along Ocean Front Boulevard in Santa Monica. On the eastern edge is the street. The western side ends in a steep cliff overlooking the beach. You've seen it thousands of times, no matter where you live, unless you don't watch any television or see any movies. It's one of the most frequently shot parts of the Los Angeles area. It's lined by ancient palm trees, and littered with leaves, papers and the homeless.

For a summer day, it wasn't all that crowded. Everyone was on the beach below. Bob wanted to be sure there were plenty of witnesses. I spotted Griswell near the meeting place, tossing bread crumbs to the birds. At least I was pretty sure it was Griswell. He smiled and nodded at us, and he was wearing a purple Hawaiian shirt with tan polyester slacks, as he said he would be. He was also within earshot, which was the point.

Oakes was right on time. He wore a tweed sport coat, plenty ridiculous on a summer Saturday next to the beach. It also bulged near his left hip. I have no idea who that idiot thought he was fooling. I suppose since he thought he was meeting members of a dangerous cult, he felt he needed something big to defend himself from the godless fiends.

"Why's his jacket sticking out like that?" Bob asked me softly. Okay. He fooled Bob.

"It's a hand gun, probably a three fifty seven magnum, at the very smallest."

"Son of a bitch."

Bob started a retreat, but Oakes had spotted him.

"You, there," Oakes demanded. "I know who you say you are. What do you want?"

"Don't come any closer," Bob called when Oakes was about ten yards away. "There is a little girl who was entrusted to us by Children's Services of Los Angeles County. We know you have her. We just want you to give her back to us."

Oakes laughed. "The child is being cared for in a Christian home. I cannot in good conscience turn her over to non-Christians, especially ones who belong to a religious cult."

"We do not belong any cult," said Bob. "And we are Christians, unless, of course, you're down on Catholics, too."

"I don't need to listen to your lies," said Oakes.

"Then how about the truth? And how about Patricia Halford? We know you had her, too. And we also know what you did to her, starting with kidnapping. We've got a positive ID on that light Mercedes of yours. How do you think we found you?"

That got him.

Bob grinned. "We have something you might be missing."

"How did you get it?" Oakes demanded. Good. He didn't want anybody to know about the journal, either.

"Suffice it to say that we did. We'll trade. You bring us Chrissie. We'll return what you seem to be

174

missing."

Oakes had to think about this one. It took him a minute or two. I guess it wasn't something he was used to doing.

"I cannot return the girl to a cult," he said finally.

Bob shook his head. "Oakes, you haven't got a clue about the Temple of New Jerusalem, have you? They're real easy to spot, and we don't look like them. In fact, they're all around us now."

Well, there were only four cheap polyester suits, but they did have us surrounded. They pressed in on Oakes. Dumb move. Okay, Oakes fooled them, too.

In that split second, it became very obvious to me that Oakes was going to start shooting. Funny how time all of a sudden slowed down to the crawl of your worst nightmare. Obviously, I survived. Bob still says what I did was massively stupid. I say if I hadn't, Oakes would have been up for murder two at the least, probably with multiple charges (one per body).

I charged him. He reached across his body for the bulge under his sport coat. I crashed against one cheap suit, knocking him sideways. Getting my balance didn't do much good. I don't remember hearing the crash of the gun. I was too busy reaching for it, to knock it away.

It burned. I remember that. It burned badly. Tubes, Bob's lips on my fingers, my mom crying, a siren somewhere, all faded and mixed up in some bizarre dream, then a comforting blackness.

CHAPTER EIGHTEEN

It's September now. School started about a week ago. I was pretty much back on my feet by mid-August, and now I'm back in fighting trim.

Things have been a little weird, though. As soon as I was on my feet, Bob and I started going out with Angela Jackson and Merritt Iler. Then Bob invited Janet and Dick Levy along. All six of us hit it off just dandy, and we've been moving in a pack ever since. It's a real couples thing, but I'm getting to like it.

The problem is, I've now got Angie and Janet dragging me out to the stores whenever they want to go shopping. I kind of had to go anyway. I can't say getting shot in the belly is the greatest way to lose weight, but it is effective. So, I've got a lot of new clothes, and a new hair-cut, still long, but with bangs. Bob loves the new look, and tells me so frequently, which is probably why I hassle out what to wear every morning now.

They liked it at school, too. The first day I was back I had my hair curled, and wore a full skirt with a blouse and vest. Some of the kids didn't even recognize me, and thought I was just another sub.

"Thought you'd escaped, huh?" I teased them as the bell rang.

They groaned.

"Well, gang, too bad. It's the new and improved, leaner, meaner Ms. Finnegan. And to celebrate, I've got all new homework sheets."

They really groaned. New homework sheets meant that buying old ones to copy from would not help.

Then Ralph Adams sauntered in, attitude and all.

He dropped his tardy slip on my desk and gave me a real mean glare. This was supposed to freak me out with how tough he was.

"Thanks," I said as I filed the slip in my notebook. "You can stand at the back with the other tardies. With luck, we'll get some daesks."

Ralph went to the back. Some things don't change.

I have, though. Bob is in the Dakotas on that shoot he didn't want to do. I really miss him, and I actually told him so. It's funny how hanging between life and death can turn things around for you.

Mrs. Halford visited me in the hospital. She and her husband have official custody of Chrissie. Bob and Janet pulled an all-nighter working that one out. Mr. Halford hesitated about the prohibition on corporal punishment, but Mrs. Halford got him to see sense. They want Bob and me to stay close to Chrissie, too, which is great because she and Sweetness are still besotted with each other. They're staring at each other now, even as I write.

I went home from the hospital after a week. Mom had my apartment cleaned, and soup cooked. She was really great. She always is in a crisis. Between her and Bob, I was completely pampered.

Then I started getting better, and Mom started snipping a little. Bob brought over Rambo Kitty. He let Mom believe that teasing the big cats was a new development. He also let her believe he didn't know she was allergic to cats. It got her out of my apartment before things deteriorated between us.

"You set this up, didn't you?" I told him as I stroked Rambo's fur.

"What do you mean?" he asked innocently.

"You know my mother is allergic to cats."

"Oh, yeah. Darn. I forgot."

"Like hell." I purred as Bob snuggled in closer, then winced.

"Sorry," he said, shifting again. "Did I hit your incision?"

"No. It was just shifting. It's funny. Getting shot seems to have cleared my brain."

"What do you mean?"

"You know, the violence thing."

"Are you thinking that by getting shot, you've exorcised the demon?"

"No. I'll probably always find myself around violent happenings. But I can live with that now. It's like Sweetness. She's a perfect lamb, but you can never entirely trust her because there is something bestial and wild that will always be part of her. There's something of that in me, and I can accept that. It's okay."

"Very profound." Bob's lips nibbled on my ears. "What about other people?"

"I can accept them, too. Maybe."

"And me?"

"You are the original domestic cat. It's completely bred out of you." I squeezed his hand.

"Does this mean I get a commitment?"

"I never said I trusted you. But, between the shooting and waking up in ICU, I did have a really strange dream."

"Do tell."

"Someone was calling me. I wanted to go, and then I realized that if I did, I would never see you again." I looked at him. "So I stayed."

Bob's laughter bubbled out of him, and he squeezed me, and kissed me, and all that stuff. Euphoric, you know what I mean?

Other titles by Anne Louise Bannon

FASCINATING RHYTHM
It's murder in 1924, New York City, as Kathy Briscow and Freddie Little search city streets and speakeasies to find out who killed Kathy's boss.

WHITE HOUSE RHAPSODY
(www. whitehouserhapsody.com)
A Romantic Fiction Serial

President Mark Jerguessen is single and there's a dark secret why. His aide Sharon Wheatly loves driven, high-achieving guys, but does not want anything to do with their fame. You know there's got to be a way to get them together.

HOWDUNIT: BOOK OF POISONS
(co-authored with Serita Stevens)

The perfect reference for writers looking for realistic mayhem in their stories. The book not only provides all the facts on toxins, it indexes them by symptoms, reaction times, etc., to make it easy to find the deadly dose your story needs.

IT'S ALL ON
WWW.ANNELOUISEBANNON.COM

www.ingramcontent.com/pod-product-compliance
Lightning Source LLC
Chambersburg PA
CBHW020613120726
47905CB00003B/784